Ink Noted   2003

A Gift
of Magic

BOOKS BY LOIS DUNCAN

They Never Came Home
Ransom
Hotel for Dogs
Season of the Two-Heart
Game of Danger
Silly Mother
Peggy
A Gift of Magic

A Gift
of Magic

by Lois Duncan

illustrated by Arvis Stewart

Little, Brown and Company
Boston • *Toronto*

T09|71

Ninth Printing

BP

*Published simultaneously in Canada
by Little, Brown & Company (Canada) Limited*

PRINTED IN THE UNITED STATES OF AMERICA

For my niece
Heidi Lois Steinmetz

A Gift
of Magic

Prologue

Once upon a time in a house by the sea, lay an old woman, a special old woman who had the gift of magic.

She said to her daughter, who sat near her bed, "I leave you this house, my dear. You do not need it now, but there will come a time when you will. And I want to leave something to each of my grandchildren. To the boy, I leave the gift of music —"

"But Mother," her daughter said gently, "there is no boy. There are just the two little girls." She thought her mother's illness had made her forget.

"There is no boy now," agreed the old woman. "Soon, though, there will be. To him, the gift of music, although it may not do him much good, being as how he resembles his father. To one of my granddaughters I leave the gift of dance, and to the other — the one who looks like me —"

Her voice was fading and she named the gift very softly, but her daughter, who loved her greatly, was weeping and did not hear.

1

Nancy had been dreaming all night, and when she woke in the morning it was with the strange sensation that she had come back from a long journey, leaving part of herself behind. She lay very still with her eyes closed, letting herself awaken slowly.

On the back of her eyelids she could see her older sister Kirby in pink striped pajamas doing exercises at the foot of her bed. Brendon, in his room at the end of the hall, still slept, breathing through his mouth with a little snorting sound which meant that he was soon to waken. Downstairs their mother sat on the screened porch and stared at the sea.

Nancy pulled herself awake and sat up in bed.

"Mother's crying," she said.

"She is?" Startled, Kirby stopped in the middle of a plié, her knees bent out to both sides. "Are you sure?"

She continued, not awaiting an answer. "Should we go down, do you think?"

"I don't know," Nancy said. "Maybe she wants to cry by herself. It's awful to have people walk in on you when you're crying. They always want to know all the reasons for it and tell you why they aren't important."

To Nancy, everything was important. She was the one their mother called "our straight and serious child." She was made in all planes and angles. Her wheat-colored hair hung straight down her back, and her brows and mouth were straight lines across her face with her nose a straight line down its center. She was twelve years old, but her body was still as thin as an arrow.

"I don't want to see Mother crying," she said.

"We won't," Kirby said. "We'll thud on the stairs so that she knows we're coming and has time to mop herself up. Come on."

She came back up to a normal standing position and straightened her pajamas and went out into the hall.

Nancy got out of bed and followed her. The thought of Kirby thudding any place was incredible, Kirby, whose feet were as cushioned as a cat's. It was worth following to watch Kirby thud, even though Nancy did not at all want to see her mother weeping.

She need not have worried, however. Their mother turned to greet them as they came onto the porch. Her eyes were very bright, but other than that there was no sign of tears.

"You sounded like a herd of elephants," she said. "I was sure it was Brendon."

4

"I don't think he's awake yet." Kirby dropped into a canvas chair opposite her mother and stretched her long legs out in front of her. "What got you up so early? You're all dressed and everything. I thought you'd want to sleep in this morning after that long plane trip."

"I guess I was too excited to sleep." Elizabeth Garrett was a soft, pretty woman with a quiet kind of gentleness about her. "I wanted to see if it still looked the same in the morning light. It seems so strange to be back again in the same house I lived in as a little girl — to be sitting here on the same porch, looking out at the same sea."

"It's a bit like the Riviera," Nancy said, drawing in a deep breath of the salt air. "Not as crowded, of course, and the sand looks whiter." She seated herself on the end of the chaise at her mother's feet. "Is it still the way you remembered it?"

"It has grown up a lot," Elizabeth said. "Those pines along the driveway were only about ten feet tall when I went away. The flame vine by the door — I remember it as just a scrubby little thing when my father planted it. Now it covers the whole wall! Other than that, though, it's the same dear place. The tenants took fine care of it. I hardly dared hope to find everything in such good condition after so many years."

"I'm surprised you didn't sell the house after Grandmother died," Kirby said. "It must have been hard trying to keep it rented all the time we were away."

"Your grandmother didn't want me to sell it," their mother said. "She told me there would come a day when I would be glad to have a place to come to." There was a tenderness in her voice, a remembering. "Strange how she could have known that. She was a very special woman, my mother. There should be some pictures and scrapbooks and things of hers stored in the attic. We'll have to look through them someday."

"That would be fun," Kirby said. She liked to claim that she could remember her grandmother, though Nancy was sure that she did so for effect. Nobody could remember someone she had seen last when she was three years old. "I'm glad that we did come here. It'll be fun to stay in a private house for a change."

"You won't think so when you have to do house-work," Nancy said. "There won't be maid service or anything. We'll have to change our own beds and dust and clean the bathroom." She wrinkled her nose. "Just like people you read about in books. Still, it'll be a good experience, I guess, for a while."

"Girls — " Elizabeth drew a long breath. "I'm afraid I have to tell you something. This isn't to be — "

The stairs thumped again, drowning out her voice. It was not fake thumping this time, but the sound Brendon always made on stairs, even when he was barefoot.

He clumped through the living room and came out onto the porch, walking on his heels. His knees were bare and knobby under the edges of his plaid swimming shorts.

"What's for breakfast?" he asked.

Elizabeth's face brightened as it always did when she looked at her son. Brendon was a handsome little boy with his father's tilted green eyes, as clear and as deep as the sea. He had soft, light hair and a dimple in one cheek like an angel. It was ironic, Nancy often thought,

6

that he should look so darling and be, in reality, so perfectly dreadful.

"My hotel-raised child," Elizabeth said fondly.
"There's no restaurant service here, I'm afraid. We'll
have to get a bus into town and pick up some breakfast
there."

"Let's swim first." Brendon rocked back and forth
from his heels to his toes. "What are you girls sitting
around for? Don't you want to go down to the beach?"

"We haven't had a chance to unpack our suits yet,"
Kirby said. "I don't see how you can have found yours
so fast. It was down at the bottom of the suitcase. I bet
your stuff is all over the room."

"I'm going now," Brendon announced calmly, ignoring the accusation as though he had not heard it.
"Okay, Mom?"

"Not okay," Elizabeth said. "I don't want any of you
swimming alone. I don't know what the tides are like
now. It looks to me as though we've lost some beach to
storms, and that can mean strong currents."

"Oh, for rats' sake," Brendon said. "I've been swimming all my life."

"Yes, in hotel pools. An open beach without a life-
guard is something else again. Besides, we have things
to do this morning. We need to stock up on groceries,
and I want to look into buying a car."

"A car!" All three children turned to stare at her in
astonishment. Even Brendon, whose mouth had been
open for a roar of protest, let it close again without a
sound.

Nancy found her voice first.

"Why?" she asked for all of them. "Why a car? You can't even drive."

"I certainly can," her mother said defensively. "I learned to drive when I was Kirby's age. My father taught me. I haven't had a chance for years because we've flown everywhere and taken taxis and so on, but believe it or not, I drive beautifully."

"But to buy a car!" Nancy kept repeating the words. "We're not going to be here more than a few weeks, are we? If we buy a car we'll just have to sell it again when we leave. Wouldn't it be simpler to rent one?"

"Nancy, dear —" Their mother regarded them with troubled eyes. She turned to her other daughter. "Kirby —"

"What is it?" Kirby asked, her face going suddenly pale. "Is something wrong?"

It was a stupid question. Of course, there was something wrong. There had been something wrong for days, for weeks, for months even. Now that the words had actually been spoken, Nancy could feel, with a sick kind of acceptance, the great wave of wrongness rising higher and higher above them, ready to come toppling over to swamp them all. With a violent effort she braced herself against it and made her mind go closed.

"We were talking about the car," she said.

"And why we'll be buying it." Now that she had decided to tell them, Elizabeth was not to be turned from the subject. "Our stay here — well, it's not going to be for a couple of weeks or even months the way it usually is when we settle places. We are going to be here in Florida for a long, long time."

8

"We are?" Kirby said incredulously. Her face was blank.

"I didn't tell you sooner," their mother continued, "because I wasn't sure myself how things would be. I wanted to see the place again first. It had been so many years, and with renters in and out, it could have been in terrible shape. And I didn't know either how I would feel here. There are so many memories."

"You mean, about Grandmother?" Kirby asked.

"Yes, and your grandfather too, although he died so very long ago. I didn't know if the sadness would come rushing out to meet me as I came up the driveway." She smiled a funny little smile, reassuring on her lips but somehow not in her eyes. "Well, it didn't happen that way. It's the happiness that has stayed, all the good years and the love and the peace. I can live here and be — happy. I think."

"But Dad?" Brendon said. "What about him? How can he work here? His job is to travel all over the place writing articles and taking pictures."

"That's right," their mother said. "It is."

"He couldn't live here with us, could he?"

"No."

There was a moment's silence.

Don't go on, Nancy wanted to scream. Please, don't say anything more! But the words stayed knotted up inside her. She sat frozen, her hands clasped tightly together in her lap, while her mother continued.

"Your father is an unusual sort of man," Elizabeth said slowly. "He is a man who is made for travel and adventure. That's why he's such a good foreign correspondent. It isn't easy for a man like that to drag a family along with him everywhere he goes. He has tried — and I have tried — we really have —"

"You mean —" Kirby's eyes were wide with astonishment. "You mean, you're getting a *divorce?*"

"Yes," their mother said. "Your father has reached a point in his career where he needs his freedom. He is being offered chances to go places, to cover events, that are too dangerous for a wife and children to go along on."

"Like in war zones," Brendon said. He could understand this. He was counting the years until he too would be old enough to work in a war zone. "Will he ever come back and see us?"

"Of course," Elizabeth said. "Whenever he's in the United States, he'll come. He'll have so many adventures to tell you about, and he'll write and send pictures. Maybe you can visit him once in a while at lovely places — Zermat, perhaps, for skiing on winter holidays, or Capri in the springtime. Meanwhile, we'll live here, and you can go to school and —"

"School!" Brendon exclaimed in horror. "You mean you can't just teach us stuff at home?"

"Oh, Brendon, you'll love school!" his mother said. "And you girls will also. I could teach you well enough in the early years, but you'll have so much more fun going to a real school now that you're older. There'll be clubs and parties and football games and dances —" She turned to Kirby. "Did I tell you that there's a dance studio here in Palmelo? It's new since I last lived here, and it's supposed to be a good one. It's run by a Madame Vilar who used to dance with the Ballet Russe."

"It is?" A little color was beginning to come back into Kirby's face. The clouds moved from her eyes and light flickered across them, not surface light, but a brightness coming up from the depths. "Does she teach the Cecchetti method?"

"We can certainly find out." Elizabeth turned to Nancy and reached over to cover the clenched hands with her own. "I know this will take some getting used to. It can't help but be a shock. But your father and I — we've been talking it over for a long time now. We do feel it's the best thing —" She let the sentence fall off and plucked it up again very brightly, too brightly.

"There are so many things here to make us happy. Old friends live here, people I grew up with. We'll have a chance to put down roots. You'll get to know other children. We'll live in a real house. There's the beach — our own beach, not a resort area. There's even supposed to be buried treasure out on one of the sand bars. And we'll get a piano!" Her hand tightened pleadingly on Nancy's. "I used to take piano when I was a child. Wouldn't you like piano lessons, Nancy?"

"No," Nancy said, "I wouldn't."

Slowly she drew her hand out from under her mother's. Across from her, Kirby's eyes still glowed at the thought of dancing lessons. Brendon stood, smiling slightly, the dimple showing in his left cheek, his gaze already focused beyond the dunes to the green water dancing in the morning sunlight.

"Is that strip out there the bar where the treasure is?" he asked.

What was wrong with them? Nancy asked herself in amazement. Didn't they realize that their whole world was crumbling apart at the foundations? Didn't it matter to them that their father, Richard Brendon Garrett, was no longer going to be a regular part of their lives?

"I don't want music lessons," she cried bitterly. "I want to live the way we've always lived! I don't care if we *never* have a real home! I want to be with Dad!"

She closed her eyes tightly and reached out — out — across the miles, the hundreds and thousands of miles — to the place where their father was.

She found him in Paris. He was seated in one of the sidewalk cafés under a blue-and-red awning with a plate of bread and cheese in front of him, and in his hand was a glass of wine. His eyes were clear and green like Brendon's, and his brows were Nancy's, straight and blond, and his great handsome head was tilted sideways as if listening intently to what the man across the table from him was saying. It was a business lunch and he was getting briefed on his next assignment. There was a notebook by his plate and a pencil, but the page of the book was empty, for he had not been taking notes. His mind was away from the conversation; it was stretching out toward Nancy, toward all of them. She felt it touch her and sweep over her, painful and unsettled.

"He isn't happy," Nancy cried. "I know he's not! I bet if you phoned him right now he'd say he wanted us back again!"

"But he would never give up his work," Elizabeth said. "It's too much a part of him. And I can't follow along behind him any longer. I'm tired, dear. I have to settle. I need a home."

The tears she had not shown them on her cheeks were in her voice.

"It would take a very strong woman to stay married to a man like your father. In our case, it's like a lamb being married to a lion or a nesting pigeon to a — a — well, an *eagle!* We both of us wish things were different — that *we* were different — and we both of us love you. Can't you understand that, dear, and accept it?"

"No," Nancy said, "I'll never accept it."

She got to her feet and left the porch.

She could feel her mother's unhappiness flowing after her like a warm river, but she closed her mind against it. At the moment she had room only for her own.

2

Kirby had always danced. She could not remember when she had started, although her parents had told her that it was when she was three years old. She had got up from her nap one day and come whirling out of her room like a ballerina going onstage. During the ten years that followed it had become a part of her, like eating and sleeping and breathing. There had never been a doubt in her mind that someday she would be a professional dancer.

It came as a decided shock to learn that Madame Vilar did not wish to take her for a pupil.

"She is far too old to begin training at Vilar Studio," the woman said decidedly. "I never accept new pupils over the age of nine."

She spoke past Kirby as though she did not exist, directing all statements to her mother.

"But Kirby has had instruction," Elizabeth said. "She has attended dance seminars all over Europe."

"Seminars!" Madame Vilar made a snorting sound. "Seminars cannot take the place of regular classes. Short periods of study do not make a child into a dancer, Mrs. Garrett. The body must be trained for years."

"I have been training it for years," said Kirby. Her light, soft voice broke into the conversation with a note of certainty. "I've done my barre work every day, no matter where we were. I've studied from books. I've watched ballet everywhere there was a performance — the Bolshoi Ballet, the Royal Danish Ballet, the State Ballet at Frankfurt, the Royal Ballet, Les Ballets des Champs Elysées —"

"Which is worse," Madame broke in, "than if you had never tried to dance at all. You have undoubtedly taught yourself all kinds of wrong habits."

"If I have," Kirby said, "I will unlearn them."

Madame Vilar turned her gaze full upon Kirby for the first time. To the girl she seemed to resemble nothing so much as a black swan. Her neck stretched, long and supple, from between narrow shoulders with a fierce, dark head poised proudly at its top. Her eyes glared, sharp and bright, from beneath arched black wings of brows. She was thin everywhere except for her long, muscular dancer's legs, and although the lines in her face proclaimed her age, her body was as firm and strong as steel wire.

"Very well," she said. "Let us see what you have succeeded in doing to yourself. Pas de bourée, please. Grand jeté en tournant."

Kirby lifted her arms and moved forward. She went through the steps slowly and carefully and did them again and then again.

"Let's see you do some pirouettes," Madame Vilar told her.

She stood, watching the girl in silence as she twirled across the room.

"Don't you want to see her dance?" Elizabeth asked. "I mean, really dance to music? She can improvise so beautifully, if we could just put on a record —"

"That will not be necessary," the woman said. She turned her attention from Kirby back to Elizabeth. "You are aware, of course, that she does not have a dancer's build? I should consider it very doubtful that she will ever make a place for herself as a professional dancer."

"I see nothing in the world wrong with her build!" exclaimed Elizabeth. Her normally tranquil face was flushed with sudden anger. "If you don't want Kirby for a pupil, I will certainly take her somewhere else. I hear there is a studio in Bradenton. That isn't so far that —"

"I did not say that I would not accept her," Madame Vilar said sharply. "What days can she come?"

"I can come every day," Kirby told her.

On the way home, her mother's hands were clenched so tightly on the steering wheel that the knuckles showed white.

"What a horrible woman!" she said in a furious voice. "Imagine, not even letting you dance for her! And criticizing your figure! You don't have to go there,

Kirby. There *is* another studio in Bradenton; that's only a forty-five-minute drive away, and —"

"I want to go to this studio," Kirby said firmly. "I like her, Mother. I want to study under Madame Vilar."

That night she stood for a long time in front of the bathroom mirror. The girl who looked back at her was pretty in the same soft way as her mother, although already she was taller. She had nondescript brownish hair with a slight curl, light eyes and brows, round cheeks and a gentle, good-humored mouth.

Kirby stretched herself tall, picturing Madame Vilar's tiny swan's head, proud and fierce on the thin neck.

"She's right," she said as she went back into the bedroom. "Madame says that I'm built all wrong for ballet, and I really am."

"How come?" Brendon asked. He had come down from his room to play solitaire on the floor in the hallway just outside his sisters' door. His whole object, both girls knew, was to force them to step over his game every time they went in or out. Now he glanced up with interest. "Is it because you have too much bottom?"

"Yes," Kirby said seriously. "And my shoulders are too broad. I have too much hips, and I'm going to have too much bosom." She pulled her shirt in close against her body and stared down worriedly at the woman's curves. "I wish I were built like you, Nance."

Nancy was sprawled on her bed reading. She did not lift her gaze.

"I guess it takes a very self-centered person to be a dancer," she said. "A person who's always worrying about how she looks."

"That's not true," Kirby objected. "I'm not always worrying. What's the matter with you anyway, Nancy Garrett? You've gotten so snippy lately I'm about ready to move in with Bren."

"Like fun, you are!" Brendon said, forgetting his card game in joyful anticipation of an argument. "Do you think I want you prancing all over my room kicking at light switches? Nancy's mad because Mom's going to make her take piano lessons, that's all."

"You're both just unbelievable!" Nancy slammed her book closed and sat erect, wrapping her arms around her knees. "You're unbelievably selfish and unfeeling and — and — awful! All you can think about are your games and dancing and things when the most terrible thing in the world has happened right here in our family!"

"You mean Mother and Dad?" Kirby regarded her sister with sympathy. "It is upsetting, Nance, and sad and everything, but when you really think about it, things won't be too awfully different. We'll still see Dad when he's between assignments, and that's about all we ever saw of him anyway. During the last few years he's been zipping around from one dangerous place to another, and we've been stuck on the Riviera or someplace else touristy with Mother. We haven't been a *family* together for simply ages."

"But they love each other!" Nancy cried. "You know they do! Mother's going to be terribly unhappy living here!"

"Do you think so?"

Kirby let her mind go back to that first morning they

had gone into town together. They had stepped off the bus in front of the used car lot, and immediately a little fat man with a gray moustache had come rushing to meet them.

"Liz Burke!" he had cried. "Little Liz Burke! I can't believe it! Are you back for a visit? These can't be your children!"

"Back to stay, Mr. Crandel." Elizabeth's face had brightened with pleasure at being recognized. "I'm Liz Garrett now, and these are my daughters." Brendon had already rushed ahead to inspect the cars which were parked in long lines with their prices marked on their windshields.

The man's glad white smile had covered his whole face.

"Back to live here? How wonderful! And these great girls yours?" He shook his head in astonishment. "It seems like just yesterday when you were the age of this tall one. You came in here with young Tom Duncan when he was buying his first jalopy."

"Tommy Duncan!" Elizabeth's voice was warm with remembering. "I hadn't thought of him in years! I wonder where he is now and what he's doing? I guess no girl ever forgets her first boyfriend."

"He's right here in Palmelo," Mr. Crandel said. "Living right down the beach from your mother's house, in fact. He's the guidance counselor at the new junior high school. I guess there's something about this old home town that draws people back again."

"Well, it's *home,*" Elizabeth said. "And now I need a car. Do you think you can help me find a good one? I know so little about engines and things."

"Certainly, certainly, we'll find you the perfect car!"

Mr. Crandel walked with them between the rows of automobiles, and all the while, between comments on gearshifts and tires and power steering, the two of them kept talking about people and events of which Kirby had never heard before. For as long as she could remember in her parents' life together, it had been her father who had dominated every conversation; wherever they had gone it had been his dynamic personality and great booming laugh that had filled the world, with her mother soft and smiling in the background. Now here was this little man with the gray hair who did not even mention Richard Garrett. He made it seem as though Elizabeth were a kind of princess come back to visit a kingdom that she had left too quickly.

They completed the morning by buying a four-year-old Ford Fairlane.

"Our first car," Brendon grumbled disgustedly, "and it's just an old secondhand nothing. You might at least have got us that Oldsmobile Toronado with the front-wheel drive!"

But Kirby, glancing across at her mother in the driver's seat, had felt nothing but pleasure in the car and in its driver. Elizabeth might not have driven for a long time, but there was no uncertainty about her as she shifted gears and pressed the accelerator to bring the engine to life. There was a proud little smile on her face as she turned off the main street of town onto the shore road which led to their house on the beach.

"I knew I could still do it," she said softly.

Now, in the face of Nancy's misery, Kirby tried to think of some way she could bring back her feelings of that moment and make her sister understand them. It was as though a special part of her mother had lain sleeping for years and years in the shadow of someone else and was now slowly coming awake.

"Maybe Mother needs to be herself," Kirby said slowly, "more than she needs to be Mrs. Richard Garrett. Being in love isn't everything, Nance. I couldn't give up my dancing, for instance, ever, for anybody. It would be like giving up the part of myself that makes me *me*."

"That's the stupidest thing I ever heard," Nancy said flatly. "Mother isn't a dancer. Without Dad she won't have anything, and I'm glad she won't. Maybe she'll miss him so much that she'll pile us all on a plane and take us back to him again."

"I hope we stay here until I can find the treasure." Brendon gathered his cards into a pile. "How about some rummy, Kirby?"

"I have to work on my rond de jambe," Kirby said. "Get Nancy to play."

"That's no fun. She always knows the cards." Brendon made a face at both sisters and then paused, catching sight of Nancy's expression. "What is it? You seeing something?"

"There's somebody at the front door," Nancy said. "A man. He's starting to — "

The doorbell rang. Their mother's footsteps tapped lightly across the hardwood floor of the living room as she went to answer it.

They heard the door being opened.

"Why, Tom! Tommy Duncan!" Elizabeth's voice

rang out in a little cry of welcome. "How wonderful to see you! I didn't hear your car!"

"I didn't bring it," a man's voice answered. "I walked up by the beach. I ran into old man Crandel up town the other day, and he told me you were back home again. I couldn't believe it!"

"It's true," Elizabeth said. "Come on in, Tom! Don't just stand there." There was a sound of the front door closing as their mother drew her guest into the living room.

"Children! Children, hurry down here! I want you to meet an old friend of mine!"

By the time Kirby reached the top of the stairs, her mother was standing at the foot of them, looking up expectantly. Beside her was a thin, sandy-haired man with glasses.

"Good grief, Liz," he exclaimed in a stunned voice as he caught his first glimpse of Kirby. "She looks like you twenty years ago! Taller, maybe, but the same face — the same smile —"

"And this is Brendon!" Elizabeth smiled as her son shoved his way past Kirby and started thudding down the stairs to what he evidently assumed would be the serving of refreshments.

For a moment longer Elizabeth stood, still gazing upward, waiting for the third figure to appear.

Finally she said, "My other daughter must be reading. She never hears anything when she's deep in a book. Go drag Nancy out, will you, Kirby dear? I want Mr. Duncan to meet all of you."

Kirby turned and went back down the hall to the

bedroom. Nancy was still seated on her bed, glaring defiantly.

"I am not going to go downstairs," she said in a harsh whisper. "Not until that man is out of there. And if you have any sense, you won't go down either."

"Why ever not?" Kirby asked in bewilderment. "He's just an old friend of Mother's. Nance, for goodness sake, what's got into you? I've never seen you act like this!"

"Kirby, I feel it!" Nancy's voice was shaking. "I felt it the moment he came to the door! He's *not* just an old friend. He's something different. There's a different feeling about him than about anybody — anybody — who's ever come into our lives before!"

"What kind of feeling?" Kirby asked. "He looks pleasant enough. Ordinary — and kind of skinny and — oh, Nance, don't be such a nut. Come on down and meet him. He is Mother's guest, and we've got to be polite. He won't be staying long. It's too late in the evening."

Slowly, reluctantly, Nancy got to her feet.

"That's what you think," she said in a tragic voice. "Not staying long, is he? Not tonight, maybe, but he'll be back again, and again after that, and still again later. That's what the feeling's about." She regarded her sister helplessly. "This is a man who wants something! We just may never be able to get rid of him!"

3

By the time school was actually ready to start for the year, Brendon had worked himself into a state of happy anticipation. It was not because he liked school; quite the opposite, he disliked everything that had to do with sitting still and being quiet. Even so, he told himself, school could not possibly be more deadly than the long mornings of sitting in hotel rooms and being tutored by his mother. At school, at least, there would be other boys.

Strange to say, in his entire nine years, Brendon had never known another boy well. Through the years spent in various hotels his sisters had been his chief companions. He was fond of them in a way, but the largest part of the time they drove him out of his mind. Kirby was always springing about on her toes and Nancy was always frowning into a book.

There was something about the sight of Nancy reading with her brows drawn tight together and her long, straw-colored hair hanging down her back that made it impossible to go by without grabbing a handful and pulling. Then she would scream. There was no sound in the world that could match Nancy's scream. She would drop her book and leap at him to slap him, and he could jump aside and kick at her, and for a few heavenly moments there would be a real down-on-the-floor scuffle.

It never lasted long, however. Soon the energy would begin to pile up inside him all over again. In an hour he would almost have to go looking for Kirby and do something to her — pinch her, perhaps. Kirby never got as furious as Nancy, but it was only fair to pick on her part of the time so as not to favor one sister over the other.

Now, however, there would be school.

He pretended, of course, that he did not want to go. He knew that no normal person ever admitted to wanting to attend school. Still, it was all he could do to keep himself scowling as he climbed out of the car and faced the crowd surging up the cement steps of Palmelo Public Grammar School.

"Don't you want me to come in with you?" his mother asked in surprise. "You won't know what room you're in or anything. It's bound to be awfully confusing."

"I speak the language," Brendon said. "For rats' sake, Mom, I'm not a baby!"

"Well, go straight to the office then," Elizabeth said. "I phoned in yesterday to say that you were coming. They'll give you your room number and tell you who your teacher is. I'm going to run the girls over to the junior high school, and we'll stop back for you as soon as they are finished getting registered."

"You don't have to do that," Brendon said. "I'll walk. I know the way to the house from here. It's not so far."

"Oh, Mother," Nancy said disgustedly, "can't you see that he's just trying to be difficult? I bet he doesn't go in at all. He'll just turn around and go home as soon as we're out of sight."

Elizabeth said, "Brendon wouldn't do a thing like that!" but she sounded a little doubtful. Brendon noticed that she sat in the car and watched him until he was up the steps and safely into the building.

Once through the school door, Brendon found himself faced with a noisy, milling mob of what appeared to be at least a million children. They shouted and shoved and disappeared into doorways and came popping out again with lists in their hands. A few of them had harried-looking mothers hurrying along behind them, but most, like Brendon, were without parents.

There were signs on the walls with arrows pointing in all directions. TO THE THIRD GRADE ROOMS, they said, and TO THE FIFTH GRADE ROOMS, TO THE REST ROOMS, PTA REGISTRATION."

With a feeling of adventure, Brendon hurled himself into the swirling mob and was immediately swept along like a leaf in a river. A few moments later the door marked OFFICE swam by him to the right, and he hauled himself out and went through it into the comparative calm of a sunny room full of desks and telephones.

A woman behind the first desk looked up.

"Hello, there," she said. "Can I help you?"

"I'm Brendon Garrett," Brendon said formally. "I'm new. My mom said for me to come in here and find out where to go."

"Brendon Garrett." The woman repeated his name slowly. Then suddenly her face broke into a great smile. "Of course!" she exclaimed. "You're Liz Burke's little boy! How marvelous! Mr. Manzi said that your mother phoned yesterday to register you." Turning to the woman at the desk behind her, she asked, "Is Mr. Manzi in his office? I know he'll want to meet Liz Burke's son. Liz was always one of his very favorite students."

"He's in there," the second woman said, "with the Russo boy. Here it is only the first day of school, and he's in trouble already. He was shooting water pistols filled with ink. He got little Amy Steider right in the middle of the back and ruined her new dress."

"And he's a psychiatrist's child!" The woman at the first desk shook her head. "I wish Dr. Russo would try analyzing his own son for a change. In all the years I've been working in this school, I've never known of a child so —"

She broke off abruptly as the door to the principal's office swung open. Mr. Manzi stood framed in the doorway, and beside him was a freckled, red-haired boy with the largest ears Brendon had ever seen.

"Mr. Manzi!" the woman said quickly. "Guess who this is? It's Liz Burke's son, Brendon!"

"Well, Brendon!" The principal's stern expression changed at the mention of Elizabeth's name. The hard set of his mouth seemed to soften, and he came over to

Brendon and shook his hand. "It's good to have you with us, son. Your mother was a pleasure to all of us. It will be good to have a child of hers in school here."

"Thank you, sir," Brendon said politely. Looking at the man in front of him, he thought how incredibly old he must be to have actually been a principal here when his mother was a student.

"I think we'll try you in Miss Arnold's room," Mr. Manzi said. "That's a good, solid fourth-grade section. Your mother says this will be your first experience in public school. I hope you'll come to me if you have any problems."

"Thank you, sir," Brendon said. He was watching the red-haired boy. The boy was standing very still, and he was wiggling one of his ears. Just one. The right one. Every time Mr. Manzi spoke, the boy's ear would move up and down in time to the words.

"Greg Russo is headed for Miss Arnold's room now," Mr. Manzi continued. He turned to the boy, whose ear immediately stopped moving. "Greg, I want you to take Brendon with you and show him where the room is. And as for you, I don't want to see you in here again for misconduct. We are not going to go through another year like last year, do you understand?"

"Yes, sir," the boy said in exactly the same tone as Brendon. He smiled politely exactly like Brendon, except that he was not able to make a dimple in his cheek.

"I'm going to have to give a full report of this to your father," Mr. Manzi said sternly. "Amy's dress will have to be paid for. I hope your father finds some way for you to work off the cost of replacing it."

"Thank you, sir," Greg said. "Can I go now, sir?"

"You may," Mr. Manzi said. "It was nice meeting you, Brendon. Give my best to your mother. I hope you like it here at Palmelo Grammar School."

"Thank you, sir," Brendon said, making his voice just like Greg's voice trying to sound like Brendon's voice. He even tried to wiggle his ear, but nothing happened. Doing something like that was more difficult than it appeared.

Once out in the hall, Greg's politeness fell off him like an unwanted jacket.

"Brenda," he said. "What kind of name is that — Brenda? It's a girl's name. Are you a girl?"

"The name's *Brendon,*" Brendon corrected him. "It's an Irish name. I'm named after my dad, Richard Brendon Garrett. I'm sure not a girl. Are you crazy or something?"

"Well, you've got a girl's name," Greg said. "And you look like a girl, so pretty and nice with fluffy hair and dimples. Gosh, Brenda, I bet you are a girl and just don't know it. I bet your folks wanted a boy so they started putting boys' clothes on you the day you were born and they always told you that you were a boy, so now you even believe it yourself."

"For rats' sake!" The thought was such a dreadful one that for a moment Brendon was speechless. "For rats' sake!" he said again.

"It happens to people all the time," Greg said. "There's a name for it — trans — trans — oh, I forget — it's trans-something-or-other. My father's a psychiatrist. He knows all about things like that."

"For a psychiatrist, he's sure got a crazy son!" Brendon said hotly. "You try calling me Brenda one more time and I'll dig out all those freckles of yours and make you eat them. Then you'll be sick and throw up all over the hall."

It was a glorious reply, and Greg nodded, looking impressed. Then he said, "Brenda."

"What did you call me?" Brendon asked hopefully.

His hands at his sides were already made into fists and were starting to itch with eagerness. He saw Greg glance at them and watched his eyes brighten with the same anticipation.

Automatically they both looked up and down the hall. The door to the office was closed and the first great crowd of students had diminished, although there were still a number of people wandering up and down looking for room numbers.

"Brenda," Greg said. "Sweet little girly Brenda. Did your mama come with you, Brenda, dearie? Don't tell me she let her little darling come to school all by herself?"

"Okay for you," Brendon said, and he socked.

It was a tentative sock, a thumping kind of blow such as he might have given Nancy. It landed on Greg's chest with a plopping sound.

"My gosh, you even fight like a girl!" said Greg, and he threw his own fist out. It came crashing into Brendon with the speed and power of a bullet. The force of it sent him reeling backward against the wall.

He leaned there for a moment, gasping for breath, and then the glory of it hit him. This was really, honestly going to be a fight!

31

With a shout he threw himself onto the red-haired boy, both fists flailing. He was hardly conscious of the blows that came back upon him, so intent was he upon the ones he himself was delivering. He felt Greg's fist strike against his cheekbone, and brought his own knuckles hard into something soft. He heard his opponent gasp, and then he felt a knee come hard into his stomach. He doubled over and as he went down he grabbed for Greg's knees and brought him down also.

Twisting and punching and kicking, they rolled across the floor.

"Boys! Boys! Stop this immediately!" A woman's voice was crying to them.

Somewhere other voices were shouting.

Somebody said, "Run get the principal, quick, before they kill each other!"

Brendon felt a sharp pain as Greg's fist hit his nose, and he threw himself over, twisting with all his strength to get on top. He saw Greg's ear in front of his face and wondered if it would be fair to bite. Then he thought of Nancy — that was the kind of fighting she would do — so he let the ear go by and punched Greg's ribs with his elbow instead.

"Greg! Brendon! Break it up this minute!" Another voice rang out close behind them. A man's voice.

A hand gripped Brendon's collar, and he felt himself being lifted upward. He managed to land one final blow as Greg slid out from beneath him, and felt an answering kick on his shins.

A pretty brown-haired woman was dragging Greg to his feet. Brendon could see that her face was streaked with tears.

"I don't know what happened!" she wailed. "It's awful, just awful! Oh, Mr. Manzi, look at them! I heard the commotion right outside my door, and I opened it, and there they were, trying to kill each other!"

"It's all right, Miss Arnold. I don't think either of them is badly hurt." Mr. Manzi turned Brendon around so that he could look at him. "Will you two boys tell me what this is all about? You just met each other in my office five minutes ago. What could you find to fight about in that length of time?"

"I don't know, sir," Greg said. Greg looked terrible. His shirt was torn half off his shoulder, and his lip was bleeding, and there was a black bruise all around his left eye.

"You don't know? Of course, you know!" Mr. Manzi

33

turned to Brendon. "What happened, Brendon? I'm sure you weren't the one to start this."

"I don't know, sir," Brendon said.

He reached up and touched his nose to see if it might be broken. There was blood coming out of it, he discovered, but the bone seemed to be all right.

"I'm very disappointed in you, Brendon." Mr. Manzi sounded bewildered. "I can't believe that Liz Burke's son would act like this. As for you, Greg, you got your warning this morning. This is going to mean real punishment. An hour after school every day for a week."

"Yes, sir," Greg said. "Thank you, sir. Can we go into the room now, sir? We haven't had a chance yet to get our desks."

"You mean, they're both going to be in my room?" Miss Arnold's face turned pale. "But, Mr. Manzi, what will I do if they're at each other every day like this? Shouldn't we separate them, just for safety?"

Greg grinned at Brendon. The eye with the bruise around it was half closed now.

"Gosh, you don't have to worry about Bren and me, Miss Arnold," he said. "Bren and me were just letting out our aggressions a little. Actually, we're buddies."

Brendon grinned back. The grin hurt on both sides at the place where his mouth was attached to his face.

"I want to be in Miss Arnold's room," he said.

He felt wonderful. He felt better than wonderful. As he and Greg followed Miss Arnold into the room he tried again to wiggle his right ear.

4

After taking the placement tests required by the junior high school, Kirby and Nancy were both put into the eighth grade.

"Do you mind terribly?" Nancy asked worriedly. "I know how I'd feel if Brendon were put up with me. I'd just die."

"Well, of course — *Brendon*." Kirby gave an exaggerated shudder. "If it were Brendon, I'd die too. Can't you just imagine it? He'd come right before me alphabetically. Any classes we had together, he'd sit in front of me. He'd probably chew gum and stick it behind his ears, just to make me sick."

"I'm serious, Kirby." Nancy could not take the situation lightly. "You really don't mind? Even when you're a whole year older than I am?"

"Don't be silly," Kirby said. "Why should I mind? It

means we can split the homework down the middle and each do half of it. I'll have gobs more time left for practice."

The answer was so typically Kirby that Nancy could not restrain a sigh. She almost wished that her sister would be upset about their grade placement. At least, that would show that she had an interest in something besides her dancing.

Ever since she had started her lessons at the Vilar Studio, Kirby seemed to have stepped into another world. She rose in the morning an hour before the alarm went off in order to do her exercises before breakfast, and she rushed out of the building after school without even stopping at her locker so she could catch a bus to the dance studio.

At home she talked about "the girls in the class," but it was her ballet class she meant, not her class at school. To Nancy it sometimes seemed that in less than a month's time she had lost claim not only to a father but to a sister as well.

If school was not important to Kirby, it was very important to Nancy. She was a good student and spent time on her studies. Her mother had been an excellent tutor, and her vast background of travel plus her natural love of reading had given her a far better background than most of her contemporaries. She did her assignments quickly and easily and knew in her own mind that she probably could have gone on into the ninth grade if it had not meant passing up Kirby, which would have been unthinkable.

Still, with all her ability as a student, Nancy found

herself completely lost in the swirl of student life. She had never known many people her own age, and now suddenly she found herself thrust in a group a whole year older than herself. The boys stood a head taller than she, and the girls were beginning to fill out into feminine curves and to wear lipstick.

Beside them, Nancy felt like a stick.

"Are you sure you're in the right room?" a teacher named Miss Green had asked her the first day, regarding her with doubt. "This is an eighth-grade social studies class, you know."

"I know," Nancy said, flushing scarlet. "I am an eighth grader."

Every face in the room turned to inspect her curiously, and she felt like shrinking into a ball and rolling beneath the desk.

After class the boy who sat behind her gave her hair a tug as he followed her down the aisle.

"You'd better be nice to old Greensleeves," he said teasingly, "or she'll send you back to kindergarten."

Nancy didn't even bother to glance at him. The tone of his voice reminded her of Brendon's.

"Take your hands out of my hair," she hissed back in her most irritated-sister voice. "I just washed it last night."

The boy never bothered to speak to her again.

In fact, as the weeks went by, Nancy found that very few students made an effort to stop and talk to her. A few of the girls called "Hi" in the hallways, and there was one plump girl in her English class who always wanted to borrow paper. Aside from this, she felt as though she were invisible to everybody. They ran in cliques, predetermined the year before, and they seemed to look straight through her without seeing her at all.

At lunch periods, she and Kirby sat together. This was not very satisfactory because most of the time Kirby's mind was a million miles away. Kirby could have had dozens of friends if she had wanted them. There was something about her soft prettiness and the dreamy look of her eyes that had the ninth-grade boys jostling and shoving each other in order to stand next to her in the cafeteria line. But Kirby did not seem to notice or to think about popularity one way or another. She carried her tray from the serving counter without looking to right or left and sat with a little smile on her lips and mentally rehearsed the steps of the lastest dance routine while she munched a tuna-fish sandwich.

Bored with no one to talk to, Nancy took up her old habit of reaching with her mind to the places beyond her. She could always find her mother; that was never any problem. Elizabeth had taken a job at the Palmelo Library, and when Nancy closed her eyes and stared at the inside of her lids, she could see her mother there, sorting through cards or stacking books on the shelves.

Their mother's decision to go to work had come as a great surprise to the children.

"I always used to dream about being a librarian someday," she told them one night at dinner. "And now, believe it or not, there's an opening for an assistant in the children's room of the library. Can you imagine at my age having your very first job!"

"I think it's great," Kirby said. "But won't you be

kind of bored working in the children's room? Wouldn't it be more fun in the research section or something like that?"

"Goodness, no," Elizabeth said. "Facts are your father's area, not mine. I'd love to handle the books for children. I'm an expert on all the old fairy tales. I just adored them when I was little, and in the Children's Room I'll get to hold a regular story hour for pre-schoolers. Imagine being the one to give them their first introduction to fantasy and magic!"

"Magic!" Brendon exclaimed in disgust. "That's baby stuff. There isn't such a thing."

"Isn't there?" Elizabeth looked thoughtful. "I wonder. My mother was a highly educated person, but she believed in magic. She used to tell me there were people, some very special people in this world, blessed with the gift. I used to think —" She paused.

"What?" Nancy asked her.

"It sounds silly, I know — but I used to believe that my own mother might be one of those people. She had a way of knowing things — things that people never told her. It seemed sometimes as though she could almost make things happen. Did I ever tell you that she knew about Brendon?"

"About me?" Brendon was intrigued despite himself. "But I wasn't even born until after she died."

"That's what was so strange," Elizabeth said. "Your grandmother told me once that she was going to have a grandson. She said he would be very much like his father, except he would have something his father did not have. A special gift. Goodness, I can't even remember what it was. She was so old then and so ill, she often rambled when she talked. I didn't always listen closely."

"I wish she'd been right," Brendon said ruefully. "I wish she'd given me a talent for flying. Then I could kind of hang in the air over people's heads and drop things on them."

"That's an awful thing to want," Nancy said. "Listen to him, Mother! Ever since he started going around with that dreadful Russo boy he's been saying those awful things. I bet he means it too, he *would* drop things — rocks and ashtrays and paperweights!"

"And water bombs," Brendon said happily. "Greg knows how to make neat water bombs. He fills them with ink. He's great with ink."

"See, Mother!" Nancy squealed. "See how he is? Can't you do something about him?"

"He's only teasing, dear," Elizabeth said gently. "Boys always tease. Haven't you discovered that yet?" She never was willing to admit that Brendon was awful.

So now in the daytime, Elizabeth could be found behind a desk at the public library — and at the grammar school, Nancy could sometimes see Brendon, thumping through the halls, poking people. She seldom spent much time looking at Brendon.

Many times she tried to reach out to her father, but she was never able to find him. That once she had succeeded, but since then he seemed to have drawn further and further away. His letters came, long, interesting letters telling of the places he was seeing and the things he was doing. He was photographing a war — "a tiny war," he wrote, "between little unimportant countries, but it is not unimportant to the people who are getting shot. They suffer just as much as if it were a large war with all kinds of great decisions at stake."

"Do you think he misses us?" Nancy asked.

"I don't know, dear," her mother answered. "He's so involved, I doubt that he has the time right now to miss anyone. But I do know that he loves you."

"Do you miss him?" Nancy wanted to ask, but she did not do so. Something in her mother's eyes stopped her.

The day of Miss Green's social studies test, Nancy had been trying to reach her father. Kirby was late getting to the lunchroom, and Nancy sat by herself at the end of one of the tables, chewing her sandwiches and playing with her mind. She peeked at her mother, who was checking out books to a friend of hers, and even looked in on Brendon, who was doing arithmetic in long, sloppy columns and chewing gum.

Kirby rushed up at last, dumping her books onto the table.

"A pop quiz!" she said. "That darned woman! Honestly, Nancy — and I didn't even have time last night to read the unit!"

"You had time for your practicing," Nancy said. "You bounced around the bedroom for an hour and a half."

"Well, sure," Kirby conceded. "That's different. That's important." She collapsed onto the bench and began to unwrap her sandwich. "They weren't really very hard questions. I just hadn't read the stuff. You shouldn't have any trouble with them."

41

"I never do with social studies," Nancy said. "But Miss Green makes me nervous. She never has forgiven me for being twelve and in her class. I think it makes her feel the course is too easy if a twelve-year-old can keep up in it."

She turned to look at Kirby, and saw that she was already thinking about her dancing. They finished lunch in silence.

It was no surprise, of course, to walk into social studies class after the bell rang and find the pop quiz there waiting for her.

"Unexpected tests are one of the few ways to discover how well a class is keeping up in a subject," Miss Green informed them. "I put you on your honor not to divulge the questions to any of your friends in the classes that come later."

Nancy opened her notebook and fished in her book bag for a pen. There was nothing frightening to her about a quiz in geography, no matter how much of a surprise it was. The unit they were studying was about Europe, and the European continent was as familiar to her as her own backyard. She had read the unit chapter by chapter during the first week of school, simply for pleasure.

Now she straightened in her seat, waiting for the first question.

Miss Green referred to the sheet of paper on her desk.

"Name the countries of Europe," she read, "in the order of size."

Nancy bent to her paper. This was easy. She pictured each country as she listed it, as though reviewing the memory of old friends. She gave a special little smile as she reached Switzerland, which had always been her favorite. She thought of the greenness, the high white peaks of the Alps, the sound of cowbells ringing clear and soft through the sweet mountain air.

She completed the list and sat quietly, waiting for the next question. Everyone else was still writing. Faces around her were wrinkled into scowls of perplexity.

Honestly, Nancy thought, how could they have trouble with a question like that!

It seemed like hours before Miss Green picked up her sheet again: "Name all the bodies of water which touch the European coastline."

Another simple list, not even a long one. Quickly Nancy listed the names of the gulfs and seas. She wondered idly how Kirby had done with that one. She had been to all the same places that Nancy had, but to Kirby the whole of the continent was composed of ballet companies — the Royal Ballet in England, the State Ballet in Germany, the Opéra Ballet and the Grand Ballet de Monte Carlo in France. Whether or not she had ever noticed the bodies of water was anyone's guess.

She finished her list and went on to the next question: "Name the capitals of all the countries." Another easy one; you couldn't visit a place without knowing its capital.

The fourth question was to name the languages; the fifth, the principal industries.

So engrossed was she in trying to remember these, that she was not aware of the figure that had stopped by her desk until Miss Green spoke.

"Nancy Garrett, may I please see your paper?"

Nancy jumped, her pen bounding on the paper.

"I haven't finished yet," she said. "I'm only on the fifth question."

"So I see." Miss Green bent over to inspect the paper. "Can you explain exactly how that happens to be?"

"Why, I — I — just haven't gotten any further. I don't guess anyone else has either." Nancy glanced up at the teacher in bewilderment.

"I don't imagine they have," Miss Green said coldly. "Especially since I have only read three questions."

"You have?" Thinking back, Nancy could not remember the exact wording, but she was certain that she had heard five questions read.

"Maybe I'm wrong," she said. "Maybe I just thought you asked more questions."

Even to her own ears it sounded absurd.

"No, Nancy, you did not imagine these questions," Miss Green said. "They are exactly the questions that I asked the previous classes. I would be very interested in learning how you knew what they would be."

There was a long silence. All around them, heads were raised and turned in their direction. Thirty pens were held, suspended, over thirty sheets of paper as thirty students waited to hear Nancy's explanation.

"I — I don't know," Nancy said slowly. "I just sort of — knew. I do that sometimes. I mean, I guess things and they turn out to be right."

"How very convenient," Miss Green said.

There was a snicker from the far side of the room. Two girls exchanged knowing glances. A boy with a seat across the aisle cleared his throat.

"Nancy Garrett." Miss Green repeated the name thoughtfully. "Don't you have a sister named Kirby? Isn't she in my third-period class?"

"Yes, ma'am," Nancy said. She paused and then suddenly the significance of the question came through to her. "You think Kirby told me the questions? But she didn't, honestly. Kirby would never do a thing like that."

"Did you see your sister during lunch period?" Miss Green asked.

"Yes," Nancy admitted. "We ate together, but we didn't talk about geography. We didn't talk about anything much. We just ate our sandwiches and we were both busy thinking."

Miss Green picked up Nancy's paper from the desk.

"I do not put up with cheating in this class," she said darkly. "I realize that it can be difficult for a child of your age to keep up with an eighth-grade class, but no problems are ever solved by dishonesty."

"I didn't cheat!" Nancy exclaimed. "I don't have to cheat! I *know* the answers!"

"And evidently you know the questions as well." There was no sympathy in Miss Green's voice. "I would like to see you after school this afternoon in the counselor's office. I think that Mr. Duncan should have an opportunity to hear your explanation. I will have your sister paged over the speaker. We will see her there also."

"But Kirby can't stay after school," Nancy said. "She dances. She won't come. I know she won't."

"If she doesn't," Miss Green said, "you will both be in even more trouble than you are right now."

5

When Kirby arrived at the counselor's office she had only to take one look at Nancy's face to know that something bad had happened. Nancy's eyes were hard with a frosted, blue look, and her chin was thrust out in a way that her sister knew very well.

She's angry, Kirby thought. No, she isn't just angry, she's absolutely furious.

Aloud she said, "I can't stay long. I have a dancing lesson at four o'clock. I've already missed the three-twenty bus by coming here, and I simply have to catch the one at three-forty."

Mr. Duncan was seated behind a wide-topped desk. He looked older somehow here than he had the night their mother had introduced him to them in their own living room. His face was serious and thoughtful, and Kirby thought, whatever this is about, he's going to be fair about it.

However, it was Miss Green, glaring furiously from a chair by the window, who started talking.

"I'm afraid your dancing lesson is less important than the subject we have to discuss," she said firmly.

Miss Green's face was serious also, but there was nothing thoughtful about it. She had the kind of face that was Kirby's least favorite — not a straight-lined one like Nancy's or gentle and rounded like their mother's, but a tight, prissed little face that looked as though it had dried up and withered. Until this moment, Kirby had not noticed how unpleasant it was.

Now, when she answered, Kirby made her voice as sweet as possible.

"I do have to make my lesson," she said, "and my dancing *is* important. I will be happy to give you ten minutes, though, if I can help you. What is the problem?"

Miss Green's face prissed even more until it looked as though her mouth might never get back into shape again. It was as though she could not believe that anyone as soft-looking as Kirby could have spoken in such a way.

"Let me tell you now, young lady," she said, "that I will not stand for impertinence!"

"Kirby's not being impertinent," Nancy said. "She does have only ten minutes." She turned to Mr. Duncan. "Miss Green wants you to find out if my sister gave me the answers to the pop quiz in social studies. She thinks we cheated."

Mr. Duncan spoke for the first time. His voice was matter-of-fact.

"Well," he asked, "did you?"

47

"Of course not," said Nancy.

"Did we have a social studies test?" Kirby had forgotten all about it. The morning classes were things she dreamed away in order to reach the afternoon. "Oh, yes, we did, didn't we! The one on Europe. Why would I need to help Nancy? She's much better at schoolwork than I am."

"According to what Miss Green tells me," Mr. Duncan said, "Nancy did know the questions ahead of time. She was writing answers to questions that had not yet been asked. Her knowledge of these questions must have come from someone."

"I suppose it could have been me," Kirby admitted. "I have that class right before lunch, and I was thinking about the quiz when I came to the table. I didn't tell her though. If she got anything, it was an accident."

"You see!" Nancy gave Miss Green a glance of angry satisfaction. "See, I told you. I don't cheat, and Kirby doesn't either. I just didn't remember that you hadn't asked the questions yet. There was nothing cheaty about it."

"Now, wait a minute," Mr. Duncan said quickly before Miss Green had a chance to open her mouth for an answer. "You say that Nancy might have got the questions from you, Kirby, but that you didn't tell them to her. Can you explain that statement?"

"Nancy does that," Kirby said. "She always has. It's — well, a sort of hobby. She likes to do things with her mind."

"If you think that any intelligent human being can

accept that —" Miss Green began furiously, but Mr. Duncan raised a hand to stop her.

"Wait," he said. "Now, let's wait a minute, Miss Green. I would like to hear a bit more about this ability of Nancy's. There is such a thing as extrasensory perception, you know, although we don't run into it too often."

"Extrasensory perception?" Miss Green's mouth fell open. She stared at the counselor as though she thought he had gone crazy. "Oh, come now, Mr. Duncan, surely you can't be serious!"

"Indeed, I am," Mr. Duncan said firmly. "ESP does exist. I am quite positive of it. I have known these girls' family for years, and I have often wondered if their grandmother didn't possess the gift. Now, Nancy, your sister calls this a hobby with you. Does this mean that you practice this sort of thing often? I mean, that you know things without having been told them?"

"How often is often?" Nancy asked, setting her chin in the way she did when she was going to be difficult. "You mean every hour or once a day or once a week or what?"

"May I go now?" Kirby asked, glancing up at the wall clock. "I really will miss the bus if I don't get started."

"Yes, go on along," Mr. Duncan said. His eyes were still on Nancy and he was beginning to look excited. "I've done a lot of reading about ESP. It's a real interest of mine. We have a psychiatrist right here in Palmelo, a Dr. Russo, who has done some experiments in this field."

"It's the test we're here to talk about!" Miss Green broke in. Her face was a mean little knot of frustration. "If you think I'm going to give a grade to a paper that was obviously the result of cheating —"

"Please, Miss Green," Mr. Duncan said. "We'll discuss that later. Right now, I want Nancy to tell us more about this mind-reading gift of hers."

"This mind-reading gift . . ."

The words stayed in Kirby's mind as she hurried along the sidewalk toward the bus stop.

"This gift" — what a strange thing to call it! It was Kirby who was the gifted one in the family. She was a gifted dancer. But Nancy — was it possible that Nancy was gifted also — but in another way?

The bus arrived, and Kirby climbed on and settled herself in a seat. What if Nancy *was* gifted? she asked herself, continuing the line of thinking. It was true that Nancy could do things that other people couldn't. "The phone is going to ring," Nancy would say, and Brendon, who loved to answer the telephone, would get up, and the phone would ring, and he would answer it. Or "They're all out of clams," she would say as they entered a restaurant, and the waiter would hand them the menu and say, "I'm sorry. The clams are gone."

It was strange, when you thought about it, how she could do these things, but they never *did* think about it particularly, because it was just Nancy. They took it for granted as part of her, the way they took for granted the fact that she was smart and stubborn and had blond hair. She was theirs, the family's, and they loved her and they put up with her peculiarities just as she put up with theirs. Was it possible that she had something so extraordinary that it could bring that light of excited discovery to Mr. Duncan's eyes?

ESP. Kirby had heard those initials somewhere before.

The bus slowed, and Kirby got to her feet and pulled the cord.

ESP — the letters stood for something, but for the life of her she could not remember what it was. She was still wondering about it when she turned up the front walk of the Vilar Dance Studio and opened the door, and then — as always — all thought vanished from her mind before the glorious realization that she was here — here at last — and the only part of the day that mattered was about to begin.

The moment the door closed behind her the atmosphere of the dance came sweeping over her — the smell of floor wax and sweat and fresh new toeshoes, the swirl of movement, the muted sound of music from the practice rooms.

Standing in the entrance hall, Kirby could see straight through the open door into the largest of the rooms with the barre running horizontally around the walls and the great floor-to-ceiling mirrors and the shiny wood floors. A class of little ones, six- to eight-year-olds, was just finishing a lesson. Miss Nedra, one of the youngest of the teachers, was giving the instruction and Arlene White, a delicate, pale-faced girl of about Kirby's age, was acting as demonstrator. Madame Vilar herself taught only the most advanced classes, although she often sat in the corner of the room and observed.

51

Now Kirby stood for a moment watching, remembering herself at six years old, dreaming over her first reader, already certain that the only thing in the world she would ever want was to be a dancer. Then, with a glance at her watch, she turned to hurry into the dressing room and change into her leotard.

When she emerged the baby class was over and her own group was already assembling. Madame Vilar was standing in the hallway. She was wearing the traditional black leotard, and beneath it the bones of her thin shoulders stuck out like little wings.

"Kirby," she said, "you will not take Miss Nedra's class today. Instead, I would like to see you in the third practice room."

Turning on her heel, she started down the hall.

Kirby's stomach went tight with apprehension. She had seen Madame Vilar take girls into the further practice room before. Only last week she had seen two girls from the beginning class trailing after her down the hall. The next day one of the girls had withdrawn from dancing completely and the other had dropped ballet and changed to a tap class.

Kirby felt as though she were going to be ill. She could not give up taking regular lessons now — not after waiting so long to be able to have them!

Madame did not even glance over her shoulder as they entered the room.

"Please close the door behind you," she said.

Kirby followed her through the doorway and pushed the door shut. The room was very silent.

Madame crossed to the phonograph in the corner and

flicked on the switch. Kirby watched as the turntable began to revolve and a record fell in place. The needle came down, and in an instant the room was filled with music. It was a melody that Kirby had never heard before.

Madame Vilar seated herself in a straight chair next to the machine and folded her hands in her lap.

"Dance," she said.

"Dance?" Kirby stared at her. "But how — what —"

"When your mother brought you here," Madame said crisply, "she said that you could dance. I did not wish to see you dance then. Now I do. So —" She motioned with her hand. "Dance!"

Kirby felt her panic beginning to subside. There was nothing frightening about dancing, even if it was for Madame Vilar.

"All right," she said. But she did not start.

She stood quietly for a long moment listening to the music. It was telling a story of a summer sunrise. The sky was lightening and the wind was waking. Somewhere in the music there was a bird.

Gathering her body, Kirby stood waiting as the morning came alive around her and the bird sat poised, opening its wings. Then she lifted her own arms and moved out into the morning and became it all.

Kirby's gift was that she could become with her body the thing she was hearing. It was not the way it was when she did her exercises, for then she thought about each part of herself, her arms, her legs, her feet, her head, her chest. When she danced she did not think, she merely *was*. She let her body do its own thinking,

and she lifted and flew and was the bird and was the wind and was the dawn.

The sun rose slowly against the gray of the summer sky. The wind rose and caught the clouds and stirred them awake. The bird chirped, first sleepily, then hungrily; then it burst into song. All of it happened together, faster and wilder, as the sun broke free of the edge of the earth and exploded into the sky and the clouds blew apart and the wind turned to gold, and it was no longer dawning — it was a bright blue day!

The music stopped. Kirby stopped.

The dance was finished.

She had danced hard. Her legs ached. Her chest throbbed with the force of her breathing. She looked into the mirror and saw herself standing there, panting for breath. Her hips were broad and her bust rounded and her face plump and flushed, and she was not a dawn breaking or a bird soaring. She was merely Kirby Garrett.

She turned and looked at Madame Vilar.

Slowly the black swan rose from its chair.

"You did not learn that in seminars," she said.

"No," Kirby admitted. "The positions and steps, though. I learned those."

"There have been dancers in your family perhaps?" Madame asked.

"I don't know," Kirby said. "I don't think so. I think I am the first — the only — dancer."

"So you think of yourself as a dancer?" The swan-eyes narrowed. "It takes many years to become a dancer, my young friend. Years — work — practice — heartbreak. And you do not look like a dancer. You are too tall already. Your bones are large."

"But I can dance," Kirby said. She paused. "I — I didn't mean it to sound that way," she said in embarrassment. "I didn't mean to sound braggy. I know there's a lot for me still to learn. It's just that — I know I can learn it. I *can* dance."

Madame Vilar shook her head in bewilderment.

"It is strange," she said. "Looking at you, who would guess? And with no consistent training —" She shook her head again. "It is all wrong. You are not the type. You should be thinking about school parties and boyfriends. You should be planning, perhaps, to become a secretary."

"I will be a dancer." Kirby spoke quietly, but the softness was gone from her voice. It was a voice that was older than she was, clear and strong and determined. She raised her head and met the swan's sharp black gaze with her own steady blue one. "May I go to class now?" she asked.

"No," Madame Vilar told her. "You will not go back to Miss Nedra. From now on you will study only with me."

6

They had started the boat because of the door. Greg had taken it off a vacant house. Greg had a whole collection of things he had taken off houses — doors and mailboxes and gas lamps and window screens. He kept them in his workshop which was in the back of the garage.

"Don't your folks wonder where they came from?" Brendon asked a trifle doubtfully. "After all, *eight* window screens — that's an awful lot just to have found someplace."

"My folks never go in there," Greg told him. "My dad says that every child needs privacy in his life. If they went poking around in my workshop it might give me a phobia."

It was when Greg talked like this that Brendon admired him most. He had never even heard about

57

phobias until he met Greg Russo. Now when he looked about him he saw phobias everywhere. Every time a person laughed or yelled or batted his eyes, a phobia was causing it.

Greg even knew the special names of the phobias and could use them correctly. Sometimes he spoke them right out in class.

"I understand why you become upset so easily," he told Miss Arnold. "It's simply an example of your gamophobia." And he said to Amy Steider, "A girl with haptephobia like yours is never going to get anywhere in life." Whenever he made these statements they were followed by silence because no one ever seemed to know what to answer.

The fact that Greg had privacy was something else that Brendon found strange and marvelous. Not only was his workroom private, but so was his bedroom. No one was allowed to go into it without checking with Greg for permission first. When Brendon thought about his own room and the way his sisters wandered in and out of it and how his mother was always looking under the bed for dirty socks and things, he envied Greg. At the same time, the thought of Greg's privacy made him a little uncomfortable. There was something about knowing that you wouldn't be checked on that made you feel that you had to be doing things.

Building the boat was one of them.

The first time Brendon saw the big front door leaning against the wall of Greg's workshop, he said, "What a whopper! That would sure make a swell boat deck!"

"Boat deck?" Greg regarded him with surprise.

"What do we want a boat deck for? We don't even have a boat."

"We could build one," Brendon said. "You've got the tools and stuff, and there's a lot of wood here. We'll need a boat to get out to the sandbar if we want to go digging for buried treasure."

"Why don't we take Mr. Duncan's boat?" Greg suggested. "He keeps it tied up at the dock in front of his house. He just lives right down the beach from you. I bet we could hook it one day and zip out to the bar and back in it and he'd never know the difference."

"We can't do that," Brendon said. "He's a friend of my mom's. You don't hook things from people you know."

Actually, Brendon had never had any experience hooking anything from anyone.

"Besides," he added, "it would be great to have our own boat. Think of the exploring we could do! Maybe we could even find a way to get across and into the Everglades with it."

"The screen doors would come in handy then," Greg said, beginning to catch some of his friend's enthusiasm. "They could keep the mosquitoes off."

So the boat had had its beginning. At the moment, they were installing a rudder. They were attaching it with hinges from a shutter, and it was really swinging smoothly before Brendon finally tore himself away from the workshop and started for home.

He felt good as he walked along through the gathering twilight, swinging his arms and whistling a melody he had made up himself. It was the beginning of

November, but the air was still soft, and there were a few mosquitoes humming around in it just as though it were summer. He thought about the Everglades and wondered if they ought to supplement the screens on the boat with some extra mosquito netting.

Brendon liked Florida and he was glad they had come here. He liked Greg and Miss Arnold and Amy Steider and everybody else he had met so far. He even liked Mr. Duncan, although he might have been less enthusiastic about him if Nancy had not detested him. It was always more fun to be nice to people if Nancy didn't like them.

The one thing he shared with Nancy was the fact that they both missed their father. In Brendon's case, however, the missing was less emotional. He and his father were not quite ready for each other yet, and both of them knew it. There would come a day when they would be, at which time, of course, he would leave his mother and sisters and the world of women behind him.

In the meantime, he liked where he was and the things he was doing.

Now, as he walked along the edge of the beach road, he saw the house come suddenly into view from behind its fortress of pine trees. Lights twinkled at the windows, and he realized with surprise that the twilight was fading into dark. He slowed his footsteps, holding for a moment to that first instant when the lights had come into view — to the smell of the sea and the first faint stars showing over the dunes and the welcoming house and he, Brendon, not yet there.

I don't have to go in at all, he told himself experimentally. I can turn if I want to and walk the other way. I can take off somewhere — sleep on the beach — stow away on a ship — hop on a train — anything! I can do anything! Nobody can stop me!

It was a good kind of thought and he put it into the tune he was making. Whistling louder, he swung on up the road and turned into the driveway.

There were two cars in the drive, his mother's and Mr. Duncan's. They were in the living room when Brendon entered, and another man was with them. They all turned to face Brendon as the door slammed shut behind him, and he saw to his surprise that the second man was Greg's father.

"Oh, Brendon!" his mother said, looking relieved. "I'm glad you're home. You know I worry when you're out after dark."

"Sorry, Mom," Brendon said. "Hi, Mr. Duncan. Hi, Dr. Russo. What are you doing here?"

"Hello there, Brendon." Greg's father was a short man with hair the same shade of red as Greg's except that it was beginning to gray a little along the sides. "I bet you've just come from my house. You and that son of mine really seem to have hit it off together."

"Yes, sir," Brendon said. He glanced past the grown-ups and saw Nancy. She was sitting in the corner of the sofa with her skinny legs curled up under her and a worried expression on her face.

"What's the matter?" Brendon asked. "Is Nancy in trouble?" To Brendon, "trouble" meant being found out about something.

"Of course not, Bren," Mr. Duncan answered. "Your sister is an interesting person, and I've been telling Dr. Russo about her. He would like to run some tests if she and your mother are willing."

"I don't need tests," Nancy said. Her brows were drawn together in a straight hard line. "I don't have anything wrong with me. I don't even get colds."

"These wouldn't be physical tests," Dr. Russo explained. "I'm a psychiatrist, Nancy. My whole interest is in the mind and how it works. Tom Duncan, here, knows my interest in psychic phenomena. That's why he called me after his interview with you at school the other day. It isn't often that we in this small town have an opportunity to conduct experiments with ESP."

"ESP?" Their mother looked startled. "Surely you don't think that Nancy has that sort of sensitivity?"

Brendon looked at Nancy. She was sitting very still. She was wearing a pair of faded old shorts and a sweat shirt, and except for the worry on her face, she didn't look any different than usual. Whatever she had, it did not appear to be serious.

"What's ESP?" he asked. "Can you catch it?"

"ESP," Dr. Russo said, "stands for extrasensory perception. It's a special kind of mental awareness. People who have it can sense things the rest of us can't. They seem to have control over a part of the brain that other people don't use. Science doesn't understand fully how it works, just that it does exist in various forms and degrees. There are special schools doing research on it, but so far we still know very little."

"Nancy with ESP!" Elizabeth repeated incredulously. She paused, considering the idea. "Nancy is very sensitive, it's true. There are times when she astonishes me with her feelings about things." She turned to her daughter. "What do you think, dear? Have you ever felt you had some sort of special gift this way?"

"No," Nancy said.

"The tests we would run would be very simple," Dr. Russo told them. "One of the first is done with an ordinary deck of playing cards. Without looking at the faces, Nancy would try to guess what each card was. Anything over a certain percentage of correct guesses is considered proof of extra perception."

"Nancy can do that," Brendon said. "She does it all the time. That's why Kirby and I don't like to play rummy with her."

"Ah?" Dr. Russo's face brightened. "That is just what I was hoping to hear. Do you think you could come to my office after school tomorrow, Nancy? That is, of course, if your mother is willing."

"I have a piano lesson tomorrow," Nancy said.

Brendon regarded her with astonishment. Nancy's piano lessons were on Tuesdays.

"You got your days mixed up," he volunteered helpfully. "Tomorrow's Friday."

"That's right, dear," Elizabeth said. "You are free tomorrow, aren't you?"

"I have to practice," Nancy said. "And I have homework. I've got a paper to write for English." She stopped and drew a deep breath. The reasons all sounded ridiculous and she knew it.

"Actually," she admitted in a small voice, "I just — don't want to. I don't want to go to a psychiatrist's office. It makes me sound like some sort of freak."

"You're wrong about that, Nancy," Mr. Duncan said. "It's not freaks who go to psychiatrists. It's people who need help with problems. And in your case, it's *you* who would be doing the helping. There are hundreds of thousands of dollars in this world being spent on research to discover the very things that you may already know."

"But I don't know anything," Nancy said. "I really don't. I'd flub up on your test and waste all that time."

"I have an idea," Elizabeth said. "Why doesn't Dr. Russo give the card test right here? It can't take very long. We won't be eating until later anyway because Kirby is still at her dancing class."

"I don't — I — I —" Nancy gave a sigh of surrender. "Okay. Okay, if all of you insist. But I warn you, it won't be any good. It won't work."

A few moments later she was seated in a chair at one end of the room with Dr. Russo at the other.

"Are you ready?" the doctor asked.

Nancy nodded.

Carefully Dr. Russo lifted a card from the deck in his hand and held it with its back facing Nancy.

"Now," he said, "just write down on your pad of paper what you think this card is. Is it red or black? A face card or a small one? See if you can get some inkling of the suit."

"I don't know," Nancy said. "I don't have any idea." Her voice sounded thick and funny.

"Then just take a guess," Dr. Russo said. "Write down the first thing that comes into your mind. Got it?"

as Nancy bent and wrote something on the pad. "All right, let's try another."

One by one he went through all the cards in the deck, and one by one Nancy wrote down the answers.

When they were finished, Nancy got up from her chair and handed the pad to the doctor.

Dr. Russo glanced quickly at the pad. For an instant his face fell, but he caught himself so that he did not look too disappointed.

"Oh, there are bound to be some wrong answers," he said. "It's the percentage that tells the story. I'll have to check all your answers against the cards."

"But they *are* wrong, aren't they?" Nancy asked. "The first ones?"

"I told you, Nancy, it's the overall average that counts." Dr. Russo got to his feet. "I want to thank you, Nancy, and you too, Mrs. Garrett, for your time and cooperation. I hope I can persuade you to come to my office for further experiments, but of course it is your decision to make. This has been most interesting."

"We were delighted to have you, doctor," Elizabeth said graciously, extending her hand.

Mr. Duncan got up too.

"After I take Dr. Russo home," he said, "why don't I stop at the studio and pick up Kirby? It will save you a trip, and I can drop her off on my way home."

"Why, Tom, how thoughtful of you!" Elizabeth gave him a warm smile. "That would be wonderful. And why don't you stay and have dinner with us when you get back? We have more than plenty."

During the polite good-byes, Brendon looked across

at Nancy. Her straight mouth was pulled tight at the corners, and her face was pale.

Brendon suddenly felt sorry for her.

"Maybe your answers got right further on," he said to her in a low voice. "He didn't check very far."

"Oh, they're wrong, all right," Nancy said. "No problem there."

She turned to her brother, and there was a look of pleading in her eyes.

"Please, Bren," she said, "don't ever, ever tell anybody about this today. And don't ever say that I can guess cards, no matter *who* asks you."

7

A cold snap arrived toward the end of November. The soft summer feeling went out of the air, and for three or four days the children went around in sweaters and slacks instead of shorts.

Then, as quickly as it had come, the chill vanished, and it was warmer, though not quite the same. The mosquitoes were gone and the air seemed thinner.

"This is what a Florida winter is like," Elizabeth said.

To Nancy it did not matter much whether it was summer or winter. Each day was so filled with problems that she could not have time to think about the weather. Sometimes she looked at Kirby and Brendon and wondered what was wrong with them that they could be so obviously contented in a place where she herself was so miserable.

To begin with there were the piano lessons. She was

taking them because her mother wanted her to. The old upright piano that Elizabeth had bought through an ad in the paper was exactly the kind that she had practiced on when she was a child.

"With Kirby so tied up in her dancing," she said, "it will be nice for you to have a hobby too."

So Nancy went every Tuesday to a little woman named Mrs. Nettles who taught in the basement of the Unitarian Church, and Nancy practiced an hour each day out of the pale green book with three mice on the cover.

"I feel like an idiot," she grumbled to her mother. " 'Three Blind Mice' and 'Mary Had a Little Lamb'! At my age!"

"I can understand how you feel," Elizabeth said sympathetically. "You are starting a bit late. You'll be out of that beginners' book soon, though, and on to more interesting pieces, and it does give me such pleasure to hear a child of mine playing in this old living room. It takes me back to my own little-girlhood again."

So Nancy kept doggedly plugging away, although in her heart she was certain that she would be on "Three Blind Mice" for the rest of her life.

Brendon made it worse. Every time she played a piece, Brendon told her what was wrong with it.

"You're not holding that last note long enough," he would say, or "Can't you tell that chord's wrong? You need your third finger down a note." Sometimes he simply moaned and covered his ears and said, "The whole piano's so sour it makes me sick."

Once when he said this more rudely than usual (he

made a gagging noise and pretended to stick a finger down his throat), Nancy told her mother about it.

"I can't practice with him around!" she wailed. "I just can't!"

But, as usual, their mother did not blame Brendon.

Instead she said, "Maybe he's right. It's a secondhand piano. Probably it hasn't been tuned for years."

The next day a man came out and adjusted the strings.

But worse than the piano, which was simply boring, was school. All day every day Nancy dreaded the moment when she would walk into Miss Green's social studies class. No matter how well prepared she was for her day's lesson, Miss Green would manage to find something wrong. Even when the answers themselves were right, as they nearly always were, Miss Green marked errors.

"Your *i*'s look like *e*'s," she would write on the paper, taking off five points for carelessness, and Nancy, whose handwriting was as clear and round and perfect as any page in a penmanship manual, would seethe with silent fury.

The other students in the class were noticing the teacher's unfairness.

"I've heard about her from my older brother," a girl named Barbara told Nancy. "She's been teaching here about eight million years, I guess, and she's awfully old and cranky. She always seems to choose one person out of her classes to pick on."

"Why don't you go to the counselor?" her friend Janet suggested sympathetically. "Mr. Duncan's awfully nice. All the kids like him. I bet if you tell him how things are he'll get you transferred to another section."

"Do you think he could?" For one glorious moment Nancy pictured herself in another geography class. Then she thought of Mr. Duncan, and the happy picture faded out of her mind. Since the night that her mother had invited him to dinner, it seemed as though Mr. Duncan had been coming over to their house constantly. If he wasn't picking Kirby up at the dance studio he was taking Brendon for haircuts, and one Saturday he had even driven Elizabeth to do the grocery shopping. She would *never* give him the opportunity to do *her* a favor, never, ever as long as she lived.

There was nothing she could put her finger on to explain her violent feeling about Mr. Duncan. He had never been anything but pleasant to her, or to any of them. She only knew that every time she saw him her stomach knotted up with fear and apprehension. There was something that he was offering that she would not take, and there was something for which he was reaching that she would not, would not, give.

Besides that, it was he who had started that dreadful testing business with Dr. Russo.

The doctor had phoned several days after the card test and talked with Elizabeth.

"Nancy was right," he said. "She did not score well on the test, but that doesn't mean anything. It could have been the atmosphere — having her family around her — being in everyday surroundings. I would like very much to repeat the test in the privacy of my office."

"Would you be willing to try it, dear?" Elizabeth asked, and Nancy shook her head firmly.

"It would just be a waste of time," she said. "Besides, I'm too busy."

So Elizabeth said in her polite way, "Perhaps another time, doctor, and thank you for your interest in my daughter."

"Don't feel bad, dear," she said later to Nancy. "It was a silly test anyway. I can't imagine anybody doing well at it."

"I don't feel bad at all," Nancy told her.

The next day she had gone to the library and taken out a book on extrasensory perception. She started reading it before dinner and could hardly tear herself away to go set the table. After the meal she went straight back to her room and continued reading.

By the time Kirby came up she was three quarters finished.

"Thanks for leaving me with the dishes," Kirby said, starting her evening exercises.

"I'll do them tomorrow," Nancy said, not lifting her eyes from the page.

"And the next day too. You're two behind me. Brendon did the drying and broke a bowl." Kirby glanced over with interest. "What are you reading? Oh — hey — where did you get that? It's about ESP, isn't it? Did Mr. Duncan give it to you?"

"Certainly not," Nancy said. "I got it at the library." She turned a page.

"Well, don't just sit there." Kirby went over and closed the door and came back to seat herself on the end of her sister's bed. "What does it say? Do you think you've got it?"

Nancy sighed and laid down the book. "You won't tell anybody?"

"Of course not. I never tell things."

"Yes," Nancy said. "I've got it. But good."

"Well, gosh! My gosh, Nance!" Kirby's eyes grew wide. "How exciting!"

"I don't think it's exciting," Nancy said. "I think it's awful. It's scary. Do you realize, Kirby, that I'm a weirdo? A freak? If people knew — like Dr. Russo — if they had any idea — I'd be stuck off in a laboratory somewhere!"

"You're kidding!" exclaimed Kirby. "They couldn't do that to you, could they? It would be kidnaping!"

"They've done it with other people," Nancy told her. "You should read the case histories in this book. There's a million kinds of tests they give. The card test is just for starters. They work them all out by mathematical statistics, and some people have to take them for years and years."

"What do they do that for?" asked Kirby. "What is it they want to find out?"

"Everything. What it is, why it is, the whole works. It seems like only a handful of scientists really believe that ESP exists at all. They keep trying to prove it does, and another bunch keeps trying to prove they're fakes, and the poor people who have it get caught in between."

"Well, what is it exactly?" Kirby asked. "Is there more than one kind?"

"There sure is." Nancy referred to the book. "There's

one kind called telepathy. That means being aware of what another person is thinking. Then there's clairvoyance; that means knowing when something's happened. There are two other kinds too — precognition means knowing about the future, and being able to tell when something is going to happen. Retrocognition is knowing about the past."

"Which kind have you?" Kirby regarded her sister with fascination. "Telepathy, I guess. That's how you knew the questions on that geography test. I was thinking about them at lunch, and you got them out of my mind."

"I'm clairvoyant too," Nancy said. "I can see things happening. Brendon's building a boat, for instance. In the afternoons if I reach out and look for Brendon with my mind, I see him banging away on it. And precognition —"

"You have that too!" Kirby's eyes were wide. "The way you know when a phone is going to ring! My gosh, Nance, you're a three-star performer! They could give you tests for the rest of your life and never get through with you!"

"Well, they're not going to," Nancy said decidedly. "I'm not going to let them. I'm not going to spend my life being somebody's experiment."

Kirby was silent. When she spoke at last, it was thoughtfully.

"Just how *are* you going to spend it, Nancy?"

Nancy was surprised at the question. "What do you mean?"

"It's your gift, isn't it? This ESP thing? Like my gift is dancing? I feel sometimes —" She paused.

"How do you feel?" Nancy prodded.

"This is going to sound silly. Do you remember a fairy tale we used to read when we were little about a girl with magic shoes? Somebody put them on her feet and they became part of her and she couldn't take them off again. They made her dance."

"You think something like that happened to you?" Nancy glanced down at her sister's long straight feet.

"Oh, not with magic shoes, of course. It's the thing about having been given something. I can imagine it sometimes — somebody actually having a present for me, all wrapped up, and it's the ability to dance. 'Here, Kirby,' the person says. 'Here is a special thing just for you. Work hard at it and use it.' "

"A fairy godmother?" Nancy asked.

Kirby flushed. "See, I told you it would sound silly. It is a funny coincidence though, isn't it, with both of us having special things?"

"Then what about Brendon?"

"Oh — Bren." Kirby shrugged. "You can't count him."

"It's a nice way to think about it," Nancy said, "but I could believe it more if Brendon had something too. A fairy godmother wouldn't be that unfair, to give us two gifts and not give one to him. Besides, who believes in magic?"

"Who believes in ESP?" Kirby countered. She laughed, and the laughter was good, for it broke the tension.

74

Nancy laid the book aside and went over to the bureau to get her pajamas. Then she went into the bathroom to change so that Kirby could have the whole room for pirouettes.

As she undressed she looked at herself in the bathroom mirror. She was still straight and skinny, but suddenly, to her surprise, she saw that she was not quite as flat as she had been. She turned sideways and looked at herself again. Yes, it was true. She might never look like Kirby, but she was finally, at long last, beginning to look like something other than a boy.

She put on her pajamas and went back to the bedroom.

"Kirby," she said, "when did you first get a bra?"

Kirby was doing her pirouettes en pointe.

"Oh," she said, "years ago. I guess I was eleven. I really needed it. I was starting to flop around."

"I guess it will be years before I need one," Nancy said.

"Lucky you."

Nancy sat down on the bed to watch her sister. It seemed to her that Kirby was thinner than she used to be. The muscles stood out in long cords down her legs, but her knees were pointed and her arms were no longer so rounded. Her face looked thinner too.

"Kirby," Nancy said, "do you ever think about boys?"

"Nope," Kirby said. "No time to. Do you?"

"Boys like you," Nancy commented. "I can tell they do. They look at you in the cafeteria and smile and act silly to get your attention. Barbara tells me — you know, Barbara in my social studies class — she has a brother in the ninth grade, and he thinks you're a knockout."

"Does he?" Kirby said without interest. She was practicing on demipointe now. Her face was red with exertion and she was breathing too hard to continue the conversation.

Watching her, Nancy had a sudden picture of Kirby years from now, still stretching and bending and pointing, all the roundness and softness gone and just the muscle left.

I almost wish, Nancy thought, that she didn't have her gift. I wish she were just herself, pretty and fun and nice, without this drive in her making her go all the time. I wish she had time to like more things — pretty clothes and boys and parties and reading books and being a *sister*.

She did not say it out loud because Kirby would think she was crazy. Kirby thought having a gift was wonderful.

Well, maybe it was, Nancy thought. Maybe a person could get used to it. Maybe she would get to love being an ESP person just the way Kirby loved being a dancer.

8

Christmas began in November.

Long before Thanksgiving had appeared on the horizon, the stores were filled with Christmas decorations and counters overflowed with gay colored wrapping papers and greeting cards.

Brendon went around whistling Christmas carols, and their mother kept saying, "I don't understand it. The holidays never used to start until the beginning of December. It's been so long since we spent Christmas here in the States, perhaps I'm not remembering correctly."

Kirby did all her shopping in one afternoon the first week of December. She was not the shopping type Nancy was. Nancy could shop happily every day for a month or more without actually buying anything, just looking at things and wandering about and enjoying the feeling that eventually she would decide on something to buy.

To Kirby such shopping was a waste of time. She made her list out beforehand. When she was ready to shop she went straight to the right department of whatever store she had decided on and made her purchase and went quickly on to the next one. In one Saturday between noon and two o'clock she made all the gift purchases for the entire family, including a necktie for her father, although they were not sure just now where he was and could not mail anything until they heard from him.

She was just getting ready to leave the store when her eye was caught by something on the china counter. There, set back behind the ashtrays and half hidden by the bulging side of a huge flower vase, was a swan made of smoked glass.

Kirby crossed the aisle and stood before the counter, looking down at the small, gray figurine. It was an odd thing, delicate and yet strongly posed, the long thin neck arched back as though in anger, the wings spread wide.

A salesgirl appeared from around the corner of the counter.

"May I show you something?" she asked.

"I'm looking at that swan," Kirby said. "What's it for? It's not a vase or something, is it?"

"No," the girl said. "It's just a figurine. It's pretty, isn't it?"

"But it hasn't any purpose?" asked Kirby.

"No. It's just for decoration."

Kirby reached over and lifted the figure so that she could see the price marked on the bottom.

"That's an awful lot for something that can't be used for anything," she said.

She put the swan down again and looked at it a moment longer.

"Okay," she said.

"You've decided to buy it?"

"Yes," Kirby said. "I guess I have." She was not sure why. She had never in her life made a single purchase that had not been useful and well thought out beforehand. There was something so fierce and yet so graceful about the swan that she could not go away and leave it, lost behind the dreadful vase.

"I'll take it," she said again, "and please wrap it as a gift."

At that moment she knew that the swan was made to belong to Madame Vilar.

Kirby was dancing, Christmas week, in the *Nutcracker* ballet, which was being presented by the students of the Vilar Studio. She had hoped for the part of the Sugarplum Fairy, until she had realized that during the solo a danseur lifted the Fairy, and the only boy at the studio who was good enough to be the danseur was Jamie White. Jamie was a thin, tow-headed boy of about fourteen who had been taking dancing since the age of five. He had nice muscular legs and the scrawniest arms that Kirby had ever seen.

79

"You realize, of course, that you are too heavy to be lifted by Jamie," Madame Vilar had said in a cool, impersonal voice, and had paused, regarding her sharply, as she waited for her reaction.

Kirby nodded grimly.

"At the next recital," she said, "I won't be." She had lost five pounds in the past six weeks and was determined to lose at least ten more by the time of the Cecchetti examinations in the spring.

The part of the Fairy went to Arlene White, Jamie's cousin. She was little and thin, like Nancy, and her steps were perfect, although her dancing always seemed to have a mechanical sameness about it.

The day after the parts were announced, Arlene happened to run into Kirby in the dressing room.

"Oh, Kirby," she gushed. "I see that you're going to be the Snow Queen! Isn't that lovely! You can dance all alone without having to worry about somebody's holding you!"

"It is nice," Kirby said sweetly, "and you and Jamie will be just perfect together. I do hope there isn't a breeze that night to blow the two of you off the stage."

The other girls in the dressing room burst out laughing, and Arlene's eyes got narrow and squinty with anger.

"You don't need to be snotty about it," she said coldly. "I was just trying to be gracious. A newcomer like you can't expect to get the best part. I don't know how you got in here in the first place. Madame never takes anyone over the age of nine."

"You were being gracious?" Kirby said. "Oh, I mis-

understood then. In that case, I take it back. I hope
there *will* be a breeze that night."

She smiled her wide, sweet smile right at Arlene and
picked up her toeshoes and walked out past the laughing girls and went to the practice room for her private
lesson with Madame Vilar.

Actually, being in recital was fun no matter what role
you were dancing. The rehearsals and the costume
fittings were as exciting for a Snow Queen as for a
Fairy, and after the initial disappointment was over
Kirby began to be sorry she had been so nasty. She
watched Arlene dancing and knew that it was not good
dancing; she also knew, and this was the sad part, that
there was very little Arlene could do to make it better.
The steps were right, and the timing, and all the move-
ments, and yet Arlene White dancing was simply

81

that — Arlene White, not the Sugarplum Fairy. The magic thing that happened to Kirby when she danced, that turned her into whatever it was that the music was saying, did not happen to Arlene.

Poor kid, Kirby thought when she realized this. Poor old scrawny Arlie. No wonder she doesn't like me. If I were her I wouldn't like me either.

She decided to be nice to Arlene from then on whether she cared for her or not, and to applaud her dance as hard as she could even standing in the wings.

From the first of December on the little beach house was overflowing with Christmas. Every day Elizabeth found something new to do to make it gayer. She decorated with greens and Florida holly and had Mr. Duncan climb a ladder and string lights outside in the flame vine.

She seemed like a child herself as she rushed about hanging ribbons and wreathes and moving furniture to make room for the Christmas tree.

"An old-fashioned Christmas!" she kept saying. "In our own home! Not just some old hotel room! We'll have a tree-trimming party and go caroling and make holiday cookies and, oh, just everything! Now you children will have a chance to know the same kind of holiday I had when I was growing up!"

Nancy was sitting on the sofa examining the greeting cards which the Garretts would send. They showed a scene of a southern Christmas with a decorated tree framing a picture window that looked out at snowy Florida beaches and waving palms.

Nancy opened the top card and read the inscription.

"You don't have Dad's name here," she said.

Her mother looked up from the centerpiece she was making.

"No, dear," she said. "Dad will be sending his own cards."

"Will our names be on his card too?"

"I don't imagine so," Elizabeth said. "I think the children's names always go on the card of the parent who has custody."

There was a moment of stunned silence. It was the first time any of them had heard that word spoken.

Kirby looked at Nancy and saw that her face had gone pale.

"You mean it's final?" Nancy asked in a flat voice. "You're really divorced?"

Elizabeth nodded. "You know that, dear. I told you when I filed the settlement agreement."

"But I thought it took ages! You always read about people who are waiting for their divorces! I thought it would be years!" Nancy exclaimed in horror.

"Not in Florida," Elizabeth told them. "It differs from state to state. I thought you realized." Her gentle face filled with pain. "Please, dear, don't look so shocked. I thought you were beginning to accept the idea. I thought you were becoming adjusted."

"I'm adjusted," Brendon said. "I like living here. Dad couldn't be dragging us around with him anyway if he's taking war pictures."

"I'll never adjust," Nancy said vehemently. "Never as long as I live!"

Later that night she asked Kirby tearfully, "Are you adjusted? I mean, really?"

"I think so," Kirby said. She paused, thinking about

it so that she could be sure that she was answering honestly. "I felt funny when Mother said that word 'custody.' It was so official, sort of, and so final. But when I see the way she has settled down here, how contented she seems and how many good friends she has, I feel better about it. She fits here, Nance. She never really did trailing along after Dad."

"I don't think you love Dad the way I do," Nancy said. "You couldn't and still feel that way."

"I do love him," Kirby said. "It's just that he and Mother have made their decision, and it's their lives. It would be nice if it were different, if Dad were a quiet, settled-down sort of man like Mr. Duncan —"

"Like Mr. Duncan!" Nancy's shriek of outrage shook the room. "That's the stupidest statement I've ever heard in my life! How can you even say their names in the same breath — dumb old Thomas Duncan and Richard Brendon Garrett! I don't care if the divorce *is* final, that doesn't mean anything. People get divorced and marry each other again. It happens all the time! Look at the movie stars, they're always doing it! Once Mother sees how lonesome and miserable it is not to be married, she'll go back to Dad again! I just know it!"

"I don't know about that," Kirby said. "She seems awfully warm and contented. Like a bird that's been looking for a nest and finally found it. She's got a home, and her job, and friends, and us . . ." Her voice wandered off. Her mind had gone slipping away without her and was dancing the Snow Queen. She was leaping and whirling across a stage in a deluge of snowflakes, and her parents and Nancy and everyone else in the world were left far behind.

The weeks before Christmas were filled with rehearsals, and on December twenty-third there were two performances of the *Nutcracker*, one in the afternoon and one in the evening.

Nancy and Brendon attended the matinée. They came backstage afterward, their faces flushed with anger.

"How could Madame Vilar have given the Fairy part to that stringy girl!" Nancy exclaimed without even bothering to lower her voice. "She's crazy, that's what she is! You're a much better dancer!"

"Hush, Nance." Kirby glanced quickly around to see if her sister had been overheard. "You can't say things like that even if you think them. Madame has her reasons for the things she does. She has to make the whole show balance right."

"Oh, pooh," Nancy said. "You always think that Madame is perfect, no matter what. That White girl looks like a piece of string."

"She dances like a wind-up toy," Brendon said surprisingly. It was not a Brendon-like comment, and he had never seemed to notice much about dancing before.

They both grumbled about it all the way home, and their mother, who was attending the evening performance with Mr. Duncan, said, "Don't ruin the whole thing for me, children. If Kirby isn't upset, I don't know why we should be."

The evening performance was primarily for adults, and they did not go backstage, but waited out front in the entrance hall. Kirby changed out of her costume and hung it on a rack in the dressing room. Then she took the package containing the glass swan and left it on the desk in the little front room which was Madame's office.

By the time she reached the hall where her mother was waiting many of the other parents had already left.

Elizabeth Garrett and Tom Duncan were standing together over by the doorway. They were so engrossed in conversation that they did not see Kirby when she entered the room. Elizabeth was wearing a new red dress in honor of the season. The color was reflected in her cheeks, and her eyes were shining. She was talking gaily and animatedly, and Thomas Duncan was gazing down at her, smiling. His face held a look that Kirby could read half a room away.

Why, he's in love with her, she thought. *Mr. Duncan is in love with Mother!*

So that was why Nancy had never been able to like him! She had sensed the emotion there from the very beginning. "There's a different feeling about him!" she had cried on that first night he had come to their home.

And Mother, Kirby thought, does Mother feel it? She looks so special tonight, so bright and sparkly —

And with the thought, Elizabeth looked up and saw her, and broke off what she was saying.

"Darling!" she cried, holding out her arms to Kirby. "You were wonderful, just wonderful! You were a beautiful Snow Queen, and I was so proud of you!" Hurrying forward, she caught her daughter in a tight hug.

"She's right, Kirby. You were excellent." Mr. Duncan held out his hand. "Congratulations. I had no idea you were so accomplished."

"Thank you, sir," Kirby said as she took his hand. Then she raised her eyes and looked for a long moment at his face. It was a pleasant face, not handsome, but nice to look at. A nice, ordinary type of face with sandy hair and light eyes, true and a little shy behind horn-rimmed glasses.

She pictured her father with his great laugh roaring up out of the depths of him, the force of his personality shooting out like sparklers in all directions.

Poor Mr. Duncan, she thought. It's not fair. It really isn't.

Because now that she was with them she could see that the glow on her mother's face was for Christmas and for friendship, and for her pride in a daughter who had danced the Snow Queen. If the potential for love was there, Elizabeth still did not know it, and with Nancy so determinedly against it there was little chance that she would ever find out.

9

Brendon was the first one awake on Christmas morning. He was relieved when he opened his eyes to see that it *was* morning; he had been waking up once an hour all night just to check, and he had almost decided that some crazy thing had happened to the sun and night was going to last forever.

Now, however, he could see the furniture in his room, dim shapes in the faint dawn light, and he got up and went downstairs in his pajamas to see if he was right about what would be waiting there.

He had guessed it first when he saw the long flat box in the back of his mother's car. It was the kind of box that things came in when they had not yet been put together. Then when Mr. Duncan had come over on Christmas Eve and Brendon had been sent up to bed early, he had been almost sure.

They had not even allowed him out of his room long enough to get a drink of water.

"How is Santa Claus ever going to come if you keep wandering around like that?" his mother asked. Elizabeth still pretended to believe in Santa Claus, and Brendon had never had the heart to tell her that he had outgrown the fantasy.

Later in the evening, when the girls had gone to their room and could not tell on him, Brendon came out into the upstairs hall to listen. His mother and Mr. Duncan were in the living room, and he could tell by their voices that they were struggling hard to put the thing together.

"I think those screws go here," Mr. Duncan was saying, and his mother asked, "Then what do we use to attach this piece to the handlebar?"

I hope they got it right, Brendon thought as he hurried down the stairs. I'd hate to have to spend all Christmas morning reassembling it.

The bicycle was there in the living room, just as he had anticipated. It was a three-speed with a hand brake and a gearshift and a banana seat. Brendon examined it carefully and sighed in relief. Everything seemed to be connected correctly except for the kick stand, and he could fix that easily.

With a grin of delight he rushed back up the stairs to wake up the family.

He bounded into the girls' room and bounced onto the foot of Nancy's bed.

"Hey, wake up, you lazy dopes!" he shouted. "Santa Claus was here!"

"Oh, you nut," Kirby said good-naturedly and rolled

over and opened her eyes. Kirby always came awake quickly as though she had never been sleeping at all.

"Oh, honestly, Bren," she said as her eyes adjusted to the dim light, "it's not even daytime yet. I bet the sun isn't even up."

Nancy groaned and pulled a pillow over her head.

"For rats' sake!" Brendon told her. "You can sleep any old time! Today is Christmas!" He reached under the covers and gave her a good hard pinch, and she screamed and came up out of the pillow. Brendon leaped off the bed just in time.

Hitting the wall switch so that the overhead light would keep them from going to sleep again, he ran down the hall to his mother's room.

"Hey, Mom!" he yelled. "Merry Christmas!"

"Is it morning already?" Elizabeth blinked the sleep from her eyes and smiled drowsily at her son. Her hair was soft and mussed across the pillow, and her face, without makeup, looked too young to belong to a mother.

"We must have sat up talking too long last night," she said. "It feels as though I just came to bed two minutes ago."

"Santa's been here," Brendon told her. "I looked down the stairway and I could see the stockings by the fireplace. They've all been filled!"

"Then it must be Christmas!" Elizabeth sat up in bed and looked around for her bathrobe. On the little table beside the bed there was a small white box. She glanced over at it, and Brendon, following her gaze, said, "Is that for me?"

"It certainly isn't," his mother said firmly. She reached over and lifted the lid. The box was lined with cotton, and lying against it was a little gold heart on a chain. Elizabeth removed it from the box and raised her arms to fasten the clasp around her neck.

"Mr. Duncan gave it to me last night," she said. "Isn't it lovely? It's exactly like one I used to have a long time ago."

"It's pretty," Brendon said politely, but his whole mind was downstairs with the bicycle. "Let's go down and see what Santa brought!"

It took them over an hour to open all the presents. Brendon had been so concerned with his inspection of the bicycle that he had not really looked past it to the piles of other gifts that all but buried the lower branches of the tree.

"We've never had this big a Christmas!" Kirby said, gasping in delight over the framed reproduction of a Degas painting of a whirling ballerina who looked almost like Kirby herself. "We've always done nice things on Christmas — gone to a play or concert or something — but we've never had masses of presents."

"We were never able to," her mother told her. "With all the traveling around we couldn't carry a lot of possessions with us. Now that we're settled, I think it's time to buy some of the nice things that make a place homelike."

There were pictures for each of their rooms and books for the bookshelves. There were pink-and-white curtains for the girls' room and blue-and-green ones for Brendon's. The girls got clothes, package after package of them, blouses and sweaters and stockings and scarves. Each of them received a book from Mr. Duncan and their father had sent Swiss watches for all of them, tiny, delicate, gold ones for the girls and a husky, waterproof, shock-resistant one which could be used as a stop watch to time races for Brendon.

Kirby got a barre to attach to the wall of her room and Brendon a pocket knife, and Nancy a globe, from Kirby, and from her mother a pile of sheet music.

"That's for you to grow into," Elizabeth said when she opened the package of music. "As soon as you get out of the beginners' book, that is."

"How nice," Nancy said politely, and Brendon could not help but feel a stab of sympathy. Nancy was never going to get out of the "Three Blind Mice" book, and she knew it.

It seemed terrible to Brendon that anyone could do the things that Nancy did to a piano. She played so badly that just to listen to her was agony. The worst of it was that their mother did not seem to realize how hopeless her middle child was. She herself could sight-read, and Nancy was learning her notes, but neither of them could pick out the simplest tune unless the music was right there in front of her. Even then, when they accidentally struck wrong notes, they didn't know the difference.

After the gifts had been opened they had breakfast, a big one with pancakes and syrup, and then Elizabeth got out the turkey and began to prepare the stuffing.

"If we get it into the oven now," she said, "it can be cooking while we're at church. I told Tom that we wouldn't be eating until the latter part of the afternoon."

"You told Mr. Duncan that?" Nancy looked up from the new book that she was leafing through. "You mean, he's coming for dinner? On *Christmas?*"

"He seemed glad to be invited," Elizabeth said. "Christmas is a lonely time for people who don't have families."

"That's just it," Nancy said. "It's a family time. *He* isn't one of us. Dad's alone this Christmas. You don't seem to be worrying about *him* any."

The glowing, happy look went out of Elizabeth's face, but her voice was light and steady.

"Your father will never be alone if he doesn't want to be," she said. "He has friends all over the world who would be delighted to have him join them. If he had wanted to come here for Christmas, he could have, you know. You are still and always his children, and he can visit whenever he wants to."

"I think we ought to have Mr. Duncan," said Brendon, who always liked company. "He gave us those books, and he gave Mom that gold thing on a chain. I bet that was pretty expensive."

"He gave you a present?" Kirby said. "I didn't know that, Mother. What is it? May we see it?"

"Why, of course." Elizabeth drew out the little gold locket. She held it out on the flat of her hand so that they could all look at it. "Isn't that pretty?"

"It's lovely," said Kirby. "It's just like you, Mother, so dainty and feminine."

Nancy got up from her chair and came over to examine the necklace.

"It's a heart," she said.

"That's right."

"I don't think that's a very appropriate present to give somebody's mother," Nancy said.

"Oh, honey!" Elizabeth turned to her in astonishment. "Tom Duncan's an old, old friend! He knows I used to have a little locket like this when I was a teenager. It's gotten lost over the years — I don't know where — it was probably left behind in a hotel bureau someplace. I've always regretted losing it, and so he's replaced it for me."

"Did he give you that first locket?" Nancy asked.

"On my sixteenth birthday."

"Was he your boyfriend?"

"Oh, Nancy, really!" Elizabeth made a little gesture of exasperation. "That was years and years ago. I wasn't much older than Kirby. I've had a marriage and children — a whole half lifetime — in the meanwhile. Tom isn't anything more to me now than any of the other dear old friends from my childhood."

"Then why does he —"

The telephone rang. Nancy stopped in the middle of a sentence. A light broke through the scowl on her face.

"That —" She could hardly bring out the words. "That's — *Dad!*"

"Is it really!" Kirby was closest to the doorway and she flew into the living room. An instant later her voice rang out loud and happy. "Oh, Dad! Merry Christmas!"

"That's not fair!" Nancy cried. "I told you who it was!"

"Let me talk to him!" shouted Brendon.

They surrounded Kirby, who was chirping madly

into the receiver. She was delivering a long involved account of the *Nutcracker* and her ballet lessons and the extra instruction she was getting from Madame Vilar.

When she had finished she handed the receiver to her mother.

"Hello, Richard," Elizabeth said. "Where are you? Oh, good — that's nice. I was sure you'd be with someone." She paused and then said, "We're fine. Just fine. Yes, everybody's healthy. Have a happy Christmas. We will, thank you. Here's Nancy."

The way Nancy grabbed the receiver Brendon knew that he might as well sit down because it would be a long while before his own turn came.

When the phone was his at last, he took the receiver slowly, suddenly unaccountably nervous.

"Hello," he said.

Tiny and thin and true, his father's voice spoke to him. "Hello there, fellow!"

Across the miles and months of time between them, Richard Garrett came rushing to him, great and warm and filled with the excitement of living.

"How are you, son?" he asked. "How do you like it in Florida?"

"It's okay," Brendon said. "Where are you? What are you doing? Are you still in a war zone?"

"I'm in Rome," his father said. "But it's just for the holiday. I'll be out again tomorrow. There's a lot of political stuff going on, Bren. I won't try to go into it now. Did you get the watches?"

"We sure did," Brendon said. "Mine is great. We've

got presents for you too, but we didn't know where to send them."

"You hang onto them for me," his father told him. "We'll have a second Christmas the next time I'm in the States."

"When?" Brendon asked. "Soon?"

"Probably not till this summer. Maybe we can take a vacation together somewhere. Would you like that?"

"I sure would," Brendon said. "If we don't take the girls along we can explore the Everglades." He didn't tell him about the boat. The boat would be a surprise.

"Let me have the phone back, Bren," Kirby said, snatching at it. "I forgot to tell him about the Cecchetti exams."

"See you this summer!" Brendon managed to say before the receiver was hauled from his hand.

He turned to his mother who was standing quietly in the middle of the room, looking oddly alone there.

"He'll take us on a vacation," he told her. "In June or July or sometime."

"That will be nice," Elizabeth said. "That's a hot time in Florida. It should be good for you to get away then."

"You can come with us," Nancy said. "I know he means all of us. You'll need a vacation too, Mother." She went over to Elizabeth and took her hand. "Is he really just an old friend? Mr. Duncan, I mean? He's just like any other friend? Just someone to talk to?"

"Of course," her mother said. "I already told you that, Nance. What does it have to do with anything?"

"Then would you do something for me, Mother?" Nancy's voice was shaking. "Stop seeing him! Stop

97

having him over here! Give that locket back to him! You can take all my Christmas presents back if you'll just give me that, please, Mother!"

"But, honey," Elizabeth said helplessly, "what would that accomplish? I need my old friends now. I have to start making a life for myself, and friends are part of it."

"Just till summer?" Nancy begged. "Just till Dad comes? Oh, Mother, please?" Her jaw was trembling and her blue eyes were filled with tears.

Elizabeth sighed and put her arms around her daughter.

"All right," she said. "If it matters that much to you, darling. All right."

10

It was on a Saturday morning that Brendon was caught playing the piano. Kirby was at her dancing and their mother, who did not work on Saturdays, was out grocery shopping, and Nancy had been practicing.

Over and over she had been playing a piece called "The Lazy Pony," until Brendon, who was working on a model on the coffee table, said, "Oh, rats, Nancy, can't you put a little life into it? It sounds like the darned pony's dying."

"I'm playing it just the way it's written," Nancy told him.

"Then it's written wrong. It's creepy." Brendon got up from the table and came over to the piano. "Shove over. Let me show you."

"You can't play it," Nancy said. "You can't even read music. You can hardly even read English, judging by the grades you make."

"So what? I can hear. That's more than you can do." Brendon wedged himself in at one end of the bench and pushed until Nancy came off the other end.

Then he began to play. He played the piece all the way through, making it swingy. Then he played it again. This time he put in some different chords.

"See?" he said. "Doesn't that sound better?"

"Yes," Nancy admitted. She regarded her brother with grudging respect. "How can you do that, just pick it out like that? How do you know what notes to play?"

"How do you *not* know?" Brendon asked her. "That's the thing I can't understand. How can you sit there and keep hitting clinkers? Can't you hear how wrong they are?"

"I'm reading the notes out of the book," Nancy said. "Now get up and let me sit down. I've still got fifteen minutes of practice time to go."

Brendon grinned at her and began to play "Three Blind Mice." Every third note he hit was wrong. Even Nancy could tell that. Then he began putting chords in that went with the wrong notes, and suddenly it was a whole different song.

"That's 'Three Blind Rats,'" Brendon said.

"Stop showing off," Nancy told him, "and let me get on with my practice. I want to get through so I can go to the library."

But Brendon did not budge. He kept playing his new song louder and louder.

He began to sing with it, making his voice very high:

> *"Three blind rats —*
> *Nancy is bats! . . ."*

He was making so much noise that neither of them heard their mother's car pull into the driveway. It was not until she said, "Why, Bren!" that they turned and found her standing in the doorway, a brown paper sack in her arms, her eyes wide with astonishment.

"Why, Bren!" she said again. "Is that you playing? Good heavens, how did you ever learn to do that?"

Brendon jumped up from the bench.

"Hi, Mom," he said. "I was just goofing around. Do you want me to bring some stuff in from the car?"

"But, dear, that wasn't goofing! That was marvelous!" Elizabeth exclaimed. "Has Nancy been teaching you? Was it to be a surprise for me?"

"I haven't taught him anything," Nancy said. "He isn't reading music. He's just banging away by ear."

"But that's wonderful!" Elizabeth said. "Really, Brendon! Why, I never guessed you had talent like that! We'll have to arrange lessons for you immediately! I wonder if Mrs. Nettles can take you on Saturday mornings. That way I could drop you at the church and pick you up again after I finish the shopping."

"For rats' sake, Mom!" Brendon said in horror. "I don't want piano lessons! I don't have time for stuff like that."

"Of course you do," his mother said decidedly. "If you can play this well without having had lessons, think how beautifully you will play when you've had instruction! Why, it would be criminal not to direct that kind of talent!" She went over to him and gave him a hug. "I'm so thrilled! I just can't tell you! And, yes, you can bring in the rest of the packages, please. Just set them on the kitchen counter."

When Brendon had banged his way out the back door, she turned to Nancy. There was a look of wonder in her eyes.

"Isn't this strange?" she said. "And my mother predicted it! I'd forgotten all about that. It is just incredible."

"What do you mean?" Nancy asked her.

"Do you remember a couple of months ago when we were talking about magic, about how there might be special people in the world blessed with magical talents? I told you then how my mother had always seemed to me to be one of those people. She told me once that one day she would have a grandson. She said that he would be like his father except that he would have a certain gift, the gift of music."

"She really said that?" Nancy stared at her mother in amazement.

"She really did. It was so long ago, I'd forgotten all about it until right now. And here is Brendon with the ability to play by ear! It's like something in a fairy tale!"

"Did she —" Nancy could hardly bring out the question. "Did she — our grandmother — did she predict anything else? I mean, about Kirby and me, maybe?"

"It seems to me that she may have," Elizabeth said. "I'm afraid I didn't always listen too closely. She was old then and sick. She rambled a lot in her talking. I was so busy trying to make her comfortable and take care of her that I didn't even try to follow everything she said."

At that moment Brendon came in with his arms loaded with groceries, and his mother went with him into the kitchen to put them away.

Nancy did not go to the library that afternoon as she had planned. Instead, she thought for a long time and finally went up to the attic. It was not a real attic such as children in stories always played in. It was simply a space between the rafters and the roof, large enough for storage. There was not even proper flooring, so she had to walk bent over, balancing on the protruding beams.

At the far end of the attic there was a small window that was not made to open, and along the wall beside it were some cardboard boxes. In them were the things that Elizabeth had stored when she put the house up for rent after her mother's death.

Seating herself on the wooden support next to the first of the boxes, Nancy stretched her legs out for balance and began to investigate the contents.

This box contained clothing, dresses and gloves and shoes, an assortment of odd, old-fashioned hats, and a christening gown for a baby. The gown was yellow with age, and Nancy lifted it out carefully.

This must have been Mother's, she thought with awe, trying to imagine her mother as a baby tiny enough to fit into such a garment. Had it been used for Kirby also? Possibly, for Kirby had been born here in Florida when Elizabeth had come home to stay for a few months with her parents. Nancy, however, had been born in a little town in Germany, and Brendon in Italy. Certainly a gown like this could not have been dragged about throughout the world in waiting for babies.

I'll use it for the christening of my daughter, Nancy decided. And Kirby — but then, Kirby would probably never marry and have children. Not, at any rate, if she continued with her plans to become a professional dancer.

Poor Kirby, Nancy thought with an ache of regret, and laid the little gown carefully away again against the day when it would next be put to use.

The second box, as she moved on to it, was filled with papers. Some were legal-looking documents having to do with house payments and taxes. Beneath these were the more personal things — diaries and scrapbooks and engagement calendars and letters.

One letter flashed up at her in her father's familiar handwriting.

"Lizzie darling," it said, "my poor sweet mouse! I know how tough it must be for you stuck there with your mother so sick and the two howling babies and everything else to handle. Why don't you just hire a trained nurse to take over and come on here and join me? I've got a great new assignment to cover the night-clubs of Paris! How much more fun if you could be with me . . ."

Nancy turned the letter face down and added it to the pile of tax statements. She did not want to read it further, nor could she bear to look through the scrapbooks and diaries. The days when her mother had been "my poor sweet mouse" were now behind them. Or — were they? Surely there must be some way —

She picked up a photograph album. She opened it and smiled despite herself at the pretty girl who posed self-consciously on the pages. Elizabeth had been in her teens then, a slighter version of Kirby, dressed in sweaters and skirts that came inches below her knees and wearing, always it seemed, a single string of pearls. And lipstick, so bright across that wide, sweet mouth! And hair flattened down on top and curled at the ends like an old-fashioned doll!

The background of the pictures was familiar. It was the same house they were living in now. The trees and vines were hardly started, and the house itself seemed to be nestled between barren dunes.

There was a boy in a couple of the snapshots. In one he was dressed in a white dinner jacket and was gazing down at the young Elizabeth with an adoring look on his face. She was wearing a long fluffy dress, and there were flowers tied around her wrist, and around her neck a little locket dangled on a thin chain. When she looked more closely, Nancy recognized the boy as a young Tom Duncan.

She turned the page, and there at last she found what she was really looking for. She recognized the face as soon as she saw it. Her mother had a snapshot of her parents that she carried in her wallet, but the woman in that picture was old and snowy haired and wearing glasses.

Here in the album she was much younger. She had flaxen hair, piled high on her head, and a straight firm mouth and clear eyes that looked straight into Nancy's own.

It's true, Nancy thought in astonishment. I do look exactly like her.

She laid the album open in her lap and sat studying

the face in the picture. It was a strong face, shaped by bones instead of flesh. An intelligent face, too intense to be really pretty.

I know you, Nancy thought. I *know* you, Grand-mother.

It was a strange feeling, this knowing, this complete and absolute knowing of a person she could not even remember.

Nancy closed her eyes, and the face was still there before her, etched upon the inside of her lids. It was as though it had been waiting all these many years to come into her mind, and now it was there, and it had no intention of ever leaving.

Nancy reached out a way and stopped, beginning to feel frightened. I can't, she thought — and even as she thought it she knew that this was not true. It was there, the thing she was reaching for, right there at her mind's edge. She could, she *could*, reach out and touch it if she tried.

I'm not ready, she cried silently. Not for this! It's too soon! I'm too young! I don't know enough!

But she had no control any longer, for now suddenly her mind was moving on without her. The face on her lids was blurring, softening, shrinking with the years until it was much more like the snapshot in Elizabeth's wallet than like the one in the album.

The room was warm and close and filled with the smell of illness.

"To the boy," the old woman was saying, "I leave the gift of music."

"But, Mother!" Elizabeth took the thin old hand in

hers. "There is no boy. There are just the two little girls."

"There is no boy now," agreed the woman on the bed. "Soon though, there will be. To him, the gift of music, although it may not do him much good, being as how he resembles his father. To one of my granddaughters I leave the gift of dance, and to the other —"

"To me?" Nancy said. She spoke aloud, and she could hear her voice ringing clear in the empty attic.

Elizabeth did not turn her head, but the grandmother said, "To you, a sort of magic. Do you want it?"

"I don't know," Nancy said. "It scares me. I don't know how to use it."

"You will learn. You must learn if you accept it. A gift is nothing unless it's used. A mind must be exercised, stretched, trained to its full potential, like a dancer's body, like the hands of a pianist."

"You mean I must practice?" Nancy asked.

"More than practice. Practice is doing the same thing over and over. There must be more than that. There must be reaching. You must go out, out, in all directions, further each time than seems possible, and the next time further still —"

"Mother, dear," Elizabeth said, "you must stop talking. You must save your strength. You can tell me things later."

"It is not you to whom I am talking," the grandmother said.

"But, dear," and there were tears in her daughter's eyes as she bent to kiss the sunken cheek, "I'm the only one here. There is no one in this room but me."

Nancy opened her eyes. The album still lay in her lap, open to the picture. The light from the little window fell in a trickle across the cardboard boxes.

Nancy raised her hands and pressed them against her forehead. Her head ached, and she was tired, tired as though she had been running for miles, had not slept in months and —

And, *I did it!* The realization leapt alive in her mind, chasing the weariness like dust before a windstorm. I did it! I did it! I reached backward!

What was the word? She had read it aloud to Kirby. *Retrocognition* — a knowledge, a reliving of events past.

But surely it was not meant to be this, this mingling of past and present! Looking back, it might be. That was not too much stranger, really, than looking forward, than knowing that the telephone was about to ring and that the voice on it would be her father's. That part, the looking ahead, through seconds or minutes, had been so much a part of her for so long that she had never even had to reach for it. It simply happened, like breathing, like one foot stretching out automatically to follow the other.

But we *touched*, Nancy thought incredulously. I found my grandmother, and we touched! How could that have happened unless — unless —

"You are so like your grandmother." Elizabeth's words came back to her. She had spoken them more than once. Always Nancy had thought she meant the physical appearance.

What if it is more than that? she thought now. What if Grandmother could reach forward, into the future, and I can reach backward, into the past, and what if somewhere in between with both of us reaching — we *met!*

The whole idea was so strange that it was terrifying. And yet there had been nothing evil in the experience. It had been beautiful in its way, like opening a box and finding that it had no bottom, that you could reach down and down and down inside of it and never find it empty and never find an end.

It was quiet and peaceful in the attic. Nancy sat there and thought for a long, long time.

She thought about Kirby and her dancing, Kirby pushing her body to the furthest limits of what it could do.

She thought about Brendon, who never did anything unless he had to.

She thought about her mother.

Why not to Mother, she asked herself. Why didn't she give this gift of magic to her own daughter?

But perhaps she had tried to. Perhaps Elizabeth, "poor sweet mouse" Elizabeth, had not been able to accept the challenge of a gift so strange.

But I am, Nancy thought. *I am.*

She looked again at the picture of the woman in the album, and her own face looked back at her. The two pairs of eyes, hers and her grandmother's, met and held, and out of all the strangeness and uncertainty, Nancy knew one thing.

Whatever this power was that had been given her, it had been given out of love.

11

Semester grades were given the second week in January. Nancy's consisted of straight A's in everything except social studies, and in that she had a C.

"That's not so terrible," comforted Kirby whose own card was a blend of B's and C's. "I don't have a single A and didn't even expect one. And look at Brendon with *all* those notes from the teacher and a D in citizenship! Why, you're some kind of a paragon compared to the two of us!"

"That's not the point," Nancy said angrily. "I deserve an A in social studies! That's my best subject. I've been to all the places! I could practically have written that textbook myself." Her blue eyes were blazing. "It's that horrid Miss Green! She's deliberately marked me down. It's not because of my work, it's because she just doesn't like me!"

"You made her look like a fool in front of Mr. Duncan," Kirby said. "She's probably never forgiven you for that. She expected you to be punished for cheating on the test paper. I don't think she ever believed about the ESP."

"I don't care if she didn't," Nancy said. "She's unfair and nasty. The other kids in the room all think so too."

"You've gotten a lot of friends since Miss Green started picking on you," Kirby observed. "Barbara and Janet and all those other girls. When we first started school they never paid any attention to you at all and now they go around with you all the time."

"They're mad *for* me," Nancy said. "Kids don't like to see grownups picking on other kids. She's not going to get away with it, Kirby. I'll teach that Miss Green a thing or two!"

"That's a dumb thing to say," Kirby commented. "You can't 'teach' a grownup. She's a cranky old lady and she's just about at retirement age. Just suffer along with her for a few more months and you'll never have to think about her again."

There was something about the way that Nancy was acting lately that bothered Kirby. She had always been serious and intense by nature, but now these qualities seemed magnified. There was a permanent frown line between her eyes as though she were concentrating on the world's heaviest problems.

The change in her sister had come so suddenly and abruptly that Kirby could pinpoint it to the very day. It was the first weekend after the holidays. She herself had spent almost the entire day at the dance studio, and when she came home in the late afternoon, Nancy had been waiting for her.

"Kirby," she had said, "I need you to help me with something. Will you?"

"Depends," Kirby had said. "What is it?"

"I want to do some exercises," Nancy said, "with my mind."

"Well, start with pliés," Kirby told her, laughing, "and think about them hard — bend slowly — down, down, down —" She broke off the joke at the look on her sister's face. "Say, are you serious?"

"More serious than I've ever been in my life," said Nancy. "I want to develop my gift the way you work to develop yours. I want to be able to use it and make it just as strong as I can."

"How?" Kirby asked. She was serious too now. "Are you going to work with Dr. Russo after all?"

"No," Nancy said decidedly. "I don't want outsiders in on this. I just want to do it at home. But I'll need your help."

"I don't know what I can do," Kirby said. "I'm surely no expert. I wasn't even sure what ESP was until you started reading up on it."

"But you can help me exercise," Nancy said. "It won't take very long. We can do it in the mornings before school if you want to or after dinner at night. You're not supposed to be dancing then anyway, with your stomach full. Please, Kirby? You're the only one I can ask!"

"All right," Kirby agreed, already regretting the time it would take and yet unable to refuse.

So from then on for a short time every day she and

Nancy had closed themselves into their bedroom with pencils and paper. Kirby would sit at one end of the room with her back toward her sister and draw figures on her sheet of paper — boxes and circles and sometimes real objects like trees and dogs and houses. On the other side of the room Nancy would sit silently, her brows knitted in concentration, and then she would begin to draw too.

In the beginning the results had not been very exciting.

"Where did you get the idea for this silly game?" Kirby asked.

"It's not a game," Nancy told her. "It's one of the experiments they run with ESP people. I read about it in that book I got from the library. I'm supposed to make my mind blank and look at the inside of my eyelids and see the same thing that you are drawing."

"I don't draw well enough for you to be able to know what the things are if you do see them," Kirby commented, but surprisingly, after that conversation, she had drawn a tree and when she had looked at Nancy's paper she had recognized, not a tree exactly, but a pair of vertical lines with other lines reaching off from them with the same general shape as a tree with branches.

After that, Nancy had seemed to improve rapidly. Many times she was actually able to draw the same thing that Kirby had and even to space it on the same part of the page.

Occasionally, for an experiment, they tried it the other way around, with Kirby making her mind blank and Nancy projecting. This never got very good results.

Kirby was not able to see any images against the wall of her eyelids, and there was nothing for her to set down upon the paper.

She did have an odd, prickling sensation, however, as though something was shoving at the edges of her mind.

"I can feel you," she said. "At least, I think I can." It was a disconcerting and not very pleasant feeling to have somebody's mind poking at you. It was always a relief when the practice sessions were over and she could get to her barre work.

There was something about it that she did not like. There was something that she did not like now about *Nancy.*

"What do you mean, you're going to teach Miss Green a thing or two?" she asked warily. "You're not going to start a petition against her or something, are you? That's sort of bitter and babyish."

"What I'm going to do won't be babyish," Nancy told her.

Kirby had no desire to ask her anything more.

It was a relief, as always, to get down to the studio. There was a tap class going in one of the side rooms, and the rhythmic click of toes and heels blended with the music from the upright piano, and Miss Nedra's voice, from another room, called out positions. Kirby felt her tensions relax the moment she was through the doorway.

What Nancy does is her own business, she told herself. I just can't spend my own time worrying about it.

So shoving all thoughts but dancing out of her mind, she went into the dressing room to get changed.

Arlene was there, putting on her toeshoes. She glanced up at Kirby, and a shadow slid across her face.

"My mother wants to know how much extra you have to pay to get private lessons from Madame Vilar," she said.

"How much extra?" Kirby was surprised. She paid nothing extra, and had never really thought about it. Now suddenly she realized how strange the situation actually was. Here she was, a newcomer to the studio, studying privately with Madame, while Arlene, who had been taking lessons for eight years and who worked as a demonstrator, was still in a class.

For a moment she stood silent, looking at Arlene's discontented face. Then she said slowly, "A lot. An awful lot, I'm afraid."

"I thought you must," Arlene said. "I told that to my mother. I could be studying privately too if we had more money."

"It doesn't seem fair, does it?" Kirby said as she put on her own toeshoes. She had the satisfaction of seeing Arlene's face lighten before she got up and left the room.

Poor Arlie! It wasn't the first time she had thought it. Still, she had raised a good question — why was Madame Vilar not charging for private lessons? Kirby knew what her mother paid the studio, for she had seen the bills. It was the minimum charge for two weekly class lessons. Kirby not only had private lessons, but she went over daily after school and used the practice room. On Saturdays she brought lunch and spent the entire day at the studio.

Maybe there's some mix-up in the bookkeeping, she thought worriedly. Maybe Madame doesn't realize that we're not paying what we should.

Of course, she should ask her — but what if she asked and Madame raised the bill? Could her mother afford to pay the gigantic amount that private lessons must surely cost? She had never thought much about money before, but it did seem that money was always a problem in divorced families. She had no idea what her father sent them, but she did know that her mother's job at the library must pay very little. There were all kinds of expenses now that they had not had before, as the cost of things in the States was higher than in Europe.

I'd best not bring it up, she thought, and then she walked into the third practice room where Madame was waiting. As soon as she saw her, she knew that she could not dance a step until she had spoken.

"Madame," said Kirby, "do you know that you are not getting paid for these extra lessons?"

The woman in the black leotard regarded her in silence a moment. Then she shrugged her winged shoulders.

"You are mistaken," she said crisply. "I am not a person who gives away something for nothing. You can be assured that for whatever I do I am paid in full."

"But — but, I know —" Kirby began and then she saw that Madame had turned her head. She followed her gaze to the top of the piano where a gray glass swan glared fiercely out over the room.

"How did you know," Madame asked quietly, "that that was my final ballet?"

"I-I don't understand," Kirby said in bewilderment. "I didn't know anything. I just saw it — and — and somehow it looked like something that ought to belong to you."

"Strange," Madame said. "It is the symbol of my last professional performance. I was dancing in *Swan Lake* at the Opéra in Paris. That is when I met Charles Vilar."

"Your husband?" Kirby asked. It was hard to imagine Madame ever having had a husband.

"He was a mathematics professor," Madame said with a little smile. "Romantic, yes? A mathematics professor?"

"Well —" Kirby said hesitantly.

"Not the profession," Madame answered for her. "But the man himself — oh, that man!" Her smile deepened and the sharp face softened in a way Kirby would never have guessed was possible. "He was handsome and good and strong, a man to be dreamed of. He had been educated in America and was teaching there at a small college in the South. He was in Paris visiting his parents when I met him. He came backstage after the performance and invited me to have dinner with him and his family.

"I was twenty-six years old and dancing lead roles with my company. I had never known love before. There had been no chance for it. From the age of eight I had been studying — only studying and dancing. Charles took me to dinner that night and the night after and again the night after. For a week we saw each other, and then it was time for him to return to the States."

"And you went with him?" Kirby asked softly. She was afraid that even the sound of her voice might break the spell.

"No, I stayed with the tour," Madame told her. "I stayed for two months longer, but the dancing was not good anymore. My teachers knew it — the rest of the company knew — even the audience. My legs were dancing, my body was dancing, but not my heart. So at the end of that time I came to America and I became a faculty wife."

She laughed suddenly. "You cannot imagine what that was to someone who had lived such a different sort of life. Still, there was Charles. He made it worth it. And when he died, ten years ago, I came here to Palmelo, where we had often vacationed together, and I started my studio. I had a dream, I think, of finding someone among my students who would carry on beyond me — who would be the dancer I might have been if I had continued."

"And in ten whole years," Kirby said, "there has been nobody?"

"There has been talent, yes, but there has not been fire." The dreamy look left Madame's face, and she turned to look squarely at Kirby. "You can be the dancer that I was not, Kirby Garrett. You have the gift — the magic something — that makes the difference. And you have the thing that I did not have — the determination. There will be nothing for you, ever, except the dance."

"My sister thinks it's awful," Kirby told her. "She thinks I'm crazy and abnormal and badly adjusted."

"She is probably correct," Madame said, nodding. "Most dedicated people are all of those things and selfish besides. How old are you, Kirby? Fourteen?"

"Thirteen."

"Good. You look older. Each year makes a difference." Madame Vilar paused a moment, thinking. "You are wasting your time here in a studio like this one. You need to study someplace where there is a company connection. You have heard of Ballet South?" She did not wait for an answer. "I think you must go there just as soon as it is possible."

"Ballet South is in Atlanta, isn't it?" Kirby asked in confusion. "Then how could I go — how could I study —"

"You would live there, of course. This is one of the best young ballet companies in the country. You would attend a private boarding school which is associated with the company. You would do schoolwork in the mornings and the rest of the day there would be dancing. There is nothing there — nothing — but study and dance. After a few years, perhaps, there would be the chance to dance in the corps de ballet with the company. There are tours in the summers." She regarded Kirby questioningly.

Kirby's heart was pounding. Her face was hot with excitement.

"It would be wonderful!" she gasped. "It would be — heaven! But do you think they would take me? And the cost — it must cost a fortune —"

"There are scholarships. The school sends their representatives around the country looking for talent. One of them will be here in the spring at the time of the exams."

"Do you really think I'm good enough?" Kirby brought out the question in a whisper. "I am too big. You know I am too big. I don't look like a dancer."

"But you *are* a dancer," said Madame softly, and she went over to turn on the record player.

12

Miss Green had been absent from class the first two days of the week, and a substitute teacher had taken her place. The substitute had been young and pleasant and inclined to giggle. The contrast when Miss Green came back again was shattering.

Wednesday afternoon when Nancy walked into social studies class to find that withered, pinched-up face waiting for her, she shuddered all over.

I cannot bear it, she thought. I just cannot sit through her class one more day.

The week had been a bad one for Nancy even without Miss Green being part of it. First of all there had been a note from her father postmarked over two weeks earlier. It was addressed to their mother, but it was to all of them, and it told about skydiving. He was going to take his camera and jump from an airplane to get pictures from behind enemy lines. Another correspondent, a woman named Maggie Courtney, was going to accompany him.

A sick kind of feeling gripped Nancy's stomach when she read the letter.

"I don't like it," she said. "I don't like his doing that. Something's going to happen."

"It can't be too dangerous," Brendon said, "if some lady's doing it with him. Women don't do things unless they're pretty sure they'll come through all right."

"Maggie Courtney does," Elizabeth said. "She's a rather special breed of woman. I met her once when she was just back from doing a piece on mountain climbing. She had made the whole climb herself, carrying her own photographic equipment. Her camera fell into a crevice, and she almost lost her life trying to climb down after it. It was a terrifying story, but she laughed about it when she told it. I'd say she's a good person for your father to have with him on any assignment."

The feeling of apprehension stirred in Nancy more strongly.

"Even so," she said, "I wish he weren't going. I feel — wrong — about it. I don't know why exactly. It's just that there's *something*."

Elizabeth turned to give her daughter a hug, and there was sympathy in her voice.

"You mustn't worry about your father, Nance," she said. "That's the thing that was so hard for me to learn during the years of our marriage. You just love him and enjoy him and trust to heaven to take care of him. If you're going to worry every time he does something dangerous, you'll be a frazzled wreck."

But Nancy did worry, she could not help herself.

And then Kirby had added her own contribution to the week that was already ruined. She had come home from the dance studio Monday evening with the idea that she was going off to live at some ballet school in Atlanta.

"The Ballet South representative will be here in the spring," she explained, "to interview students. Madame Vilar feels that I could win a scholarship."

"But Kirby!" Elizabeth gestured helplessly. "You're so young!"

"Not for dancing," Kirby said. "I'm old for dancing. You have to start young, Mother, to become a professional. And I must — I *must* become one! It's the only thing I want in the world!"

Kirby's face was radiant and her voice was leaping with excitement. Don't let her, Nancy felt like screaming, oh, Mother, don't let her! Couldn't her mother see what would happen if they once let Kirby get away from them? She would go twirling off into the clouds someplace, and they would never, ever, have her for themselves again!

Why can't she be normal, Nancy thought. Why can't she be an everyday person! Why can't she giggle on the telephone and get a crush on Barbara's brother and try for the honor roll and go to parties! She could — she *would* — if it weren't for this dancing! I wish there were some way we could tie her down and never let her put on her toeshoes!

But she could tell from the look on her mother's face that she herself did not feel that way. When the time came and Kirby was offered a scholarship, her mother would let her go because that was the way Elizabeth

124

was. She would never bring herself to withhold anything from her children she thought would make them
happy.

So it was a miserable Nancy who walked into class on
Wednesday to find the substitute gone and Miss Green
glaring out from behind her desk.

Oh, no, Nancy thought. I can't take it. I just cannot
take it.

She took her seat with a sigh, and the boy in the seat
behind her leaned forward and gave her hair a tug.

"I see old Greensleeves is back with us," he whispered. "I wonder what was wrong with her Monday
and Tuesday."

"She couldn't have been sick," muttered Janet from
across the aisle. "She's too mean to be sick."

"She was, though," said Nancy. It was at that moment that the idea began to come to her. She had told
Kirby that she would "teach Miss Green a thing or
two," but the statement had been made in anger. She
had not known at the time she made it exactly how she
would carry out her threat. Now she did know, and
suddenly she was filled with a dawning sense of excitement.

"She has a disease," she said in a low voice to the
classmates within hearing range. "She has something
called dropsy."

"Dropsy?" Barbara glanced up from her own seat
where she was belatedly trying to finish her homework.
"Is it catching?"

"I've heard of it somewhere," Janet said. "Don't you
swell up or something?"

"Children!" Miss Green's voice broke through the whispered conversation.

"The bell hasn't even rung yet," grumbled the boy behind Nancy. "For Pete's sake, we can talk until the bell rings!"

"Mean old witch," mouthed Janet silently, and Nancy nodded in agreement.

The bell rang.

Miss Green spoke sharply. "Nancy Garrett, I will have no whispering in this classroom!"

"I wasn't whispering," Nancy said. "I was just nodding my head. And anyway, class hadn't started."

"Nor will I have back talk!" Miss Green's voice was icy. "I have not been well, and I am not in any state to put up with insolence. If I hear one more word, I shall ask you to leave the classroom. If your desire is to bring up your grade this next semester, I would not advise this as a way of starting."

Nancy dropped her head and stared down at her hands which were gripped into a knot in her lap. She was so angry that she felt herself shaking. Her jaw ached with the effort she was making to keep from shouting in outrage.

All right, she thought, you've asked for it! You've really asked for it!

For the first time in her life she focused her mind hard upon a person who was not a member of her family.

She would never have attempted it a month ago or even contemplated the fact that it might be possible. A mind was a thing to look with, not something with which you did things. Yet during the past weeks of

126

working with Kirby a strange realization had begun to come to her. Sometimes it seemed to her that she had a picture in her mind even before Kirby started drawing. Instead of opening her mind to receive, she would be pressing it outward at her sister. Without even realizing it, Kirby's fingers would begin sketching the very image that was in Nancy's mind.

She had not told this to Kirby. Kirby would certainly not have liked it and might even have insisted on stopping the exercise sessions completely.

Now Nancy sat quiet, focusing her gaze and thoughts upon Miss Green. The teacher had finished her attendance check and had picked up a textbook.

"I left lesson plans," she was saying, "for Monday and Tuesday. If your substitute followed them you should be ready for a quiz today. If you will get out your notebooks —"

Suddenly, as if of its own volition, the book slid from her hand and fell to the floor.

Miss Green retrieved it and continued.

"— your notebooks and pencils —"

Her hand seemed to shake, and the book fell again.

This time she bent stiffly and laid it carefully upon her desk. Then she picked up a piece of chalk and turned to the blackboard. Her strokes were swift and angry, and the chalk made a squeaky sound.

"What are the principal products," she wrote, "of the country of —"

The chalk fell out of her hand and struck the floor.

From somewhere at the back of the room there came a giggle. It was a nervous, high-pitched sound that was contagious.

Placing one hand on the edge of the desk to steady herself, Miss Green bent once more and picked up the chalk. As she started to straighten, it flipped from her fingers. When it landed this time, it broke into pieces which went rolling off in several directions.

Suddenly Janet made a choking sound.

"It's dropsy!" she whispered. "She really does have it, just like Nancy said!"

Barbara gave a strangled giggle.

"Dropsy!" hissed the boy behind Nancy to a friend of his sitting two rows over.

"Silence!" Miss Green said sharply. Her face was pale and she let the chalk lie where it had fallen. "You will all open your notebooks if you have not done so already. Now, write these words one hundred times: 'I will not laugh at the misfortunes of others.'"

Thirty-one notebooks flipped open and thirty-one pencils were raised to writing position. People on the far side of the room were giggling now as the word spread back to them. "Dropsy! She has dropsy!" In the row by the window there was a burst of uncontrolled laughter. Janet giggled again and pressed her hand over her mouth. Everybody in the room seemed to be strangling.

"Not one hundred times — five hundred times!" Miss Green amended angrily.

Nancy picked up her pencil and began to move it across the page. As always after a blaze of temper, she felt drained and empty. She also felt shaken and oddly ashamed of herself.

I did it, she thought. I did it!

The thought was frightening.

"I will not laugh at the misfortunes of others." Her hand was trembling as she traced the words on the paper. "I will not laugh . . ."

I made it happen, she thought. I made something happen! I just thought about it and wanted it and pushed with my mind when my mind was angry, and it happened. It happened exactly the way I planned it to.

She pictured Miss Green's fingers sliding from the book, fumbling with the chalk, dropping first one thing and then another. She remembered the woman's face, white and strained, watching in bewilderment as the chalk fell from her hand.

I did it, Nancy thought, and the realization brought

no pleasure. The feeling that came instead was closer to panic. If I did that — if I could do that — then, oh, dear Grandmother, *what else am I able to do?*

Kirby, she thought, I've got to talk to Kirby! Kirby is the only one I can tell about it, the only one who knows enough to understand.

She raised her eyes to the clock on the wall. The minute hand was moving so slowly! The period had hardly started.

She looked down at the desk where her hand kept writing "I will not laugh — I will not laugh." Row after row of letters kept appearing on the paper. The words were meaningless now. Why on earth should she be laughing? To laugh was the last thing she wanted to do!

The minute hand moved, tick by tick, around the edge of the clock. The lines of "I will nots" covered one sheet of paper and another and another. The amusement of the class had died down now and the only sound was the scratching of pencils.

Nancy glanced up once to see Miss Green sitting silently behind her desk. She looked tired and old and pathetic. The chalk still lay on the floor where it had fallen.

She must think she's sick, Nancy realized miserably, or that she's crazy. And she wouldn't believe it if I told her what really happened.

When the bell rang, Nancy was the first one out of the classroom. She dropped her papers on Miss Green's desk, feeling too guilty to look at her. Behind her she heard Barbara's voice calling, "Nancy! Wait for me!" and someone else saying, "Dropsy!" Ignoring her classmates, she hurried down the hall. There was no one in the world she wanted to see and talk to now except Kirby.

Kirby's locker was at the foot of the steps in the north end of the building. By the time Nancy reached it, the hall was alive with students. They surged out of doorways and into others, bumping, shoving, calling to each other, laughing, chattering. Kirby was not at her locker yet, which was not unusual. Her fourth-period class was on the second floor.

Backing against the wall to stay out of the mainstream of traffic, Nancy trained her eyes on the stairway. Several minutes went past with still no sign of Kirby. What was taking her so long? Nancy asked herself impatiently. Was it possible she was not coming to her locker at all?

Then, as if in answer to the question, her sister appeared around the bend in the stairs. Her arms were loaded with books, and she was moving very slowly. She stopped on the landing and stood there uncertainly for a moment.

Nancy was so relieved to see her that she raised her arm and began to wave wildly. What if she weren't here, she asked herself frantically. What if she were away at ballet school. There would be nobody to talk to, nobody to share things.

She can't go away, Nancy thought. She just can't go. *I won't let her!*

At that moment Kirby pitched forward and fell straight down the stairs.

13

My leg is broken!

Kirby knew it the moment that consciousness came back to her. Even before she opened her eyes, she had to realize that the terrible pain shooting through her lower left leg could be caused by nothing less than a broken bone.

Then she did open her eyes and wished that she hadn't.

"Kirby! Oh, Kirby!" Nancy was bent over her, her face white with terror. "Kirby, are you all right?"

"Of course I'm not all right," Kirby managed to gasp.

"Oh, Kirby!" Nancy could not seem to say anything but her sister's name. Her eyes were wide and horrified, and her face was so huge and close that Kirby longed to reach up and shove her away.

"Get back now! Give her air!" another voice said

sharply. Nancy's face disappeared and was replaced by that of one of the young seventh-grade teachers. "Hang on now, dear," she said to Kirby. "Somebody has gone for the nurse. You'll be all right."

"I won't be all right!" Kirby cried. "It's my leg! My *leg!*" She knew she was screaming the words. They were one great shriek inside her. For some reason, though, she could not get the sound of them out past her lips.

She was aware suddenly that there was a whole crowd gathered around her. From her position on the floor a million legs seemed to surround her.

The seventh grade teacher was ordering people back.

"Give her air!" she was saying. "Don't let her faint again."

Then a man's voice said, "Clear the way and let me through here." The legs which had not moved at the teacher's request now began to do so.

A moment later Kirby found Tom Duncan on his knees beside her.

"Don't you know better," he asked, "than to try to dance on a narrow landing? And then to try to fly! Did you think you were the Sugarplum Fairy?"

"The Cecchetti exams —" Kirby whispered, "Ballet South — the scholarship —"

"Easy does it, Kirby." Mr. Duncan's voice was gentle. "We'll worry about those things later."

His hand closed over hers, and Kirby grasped it tightly. It was a strong hand, and when she gripped it hard the pain that surged through her seemed to lessen. She closed her eyes and clung to the hand as she was lifted onto a stretcher and into an ambulance and all the way to the hospital.

Her mother was there when they brought her back from surgery. The anesthetic they had given her still had not worn off completely.

"My leg —" Kirby murmured, and Elizabeth said, "It's broken. They've set it now, darling, and it's going to mend just splendidly."

Her face kept rippling back and forth like a flag in a wind storm. Her voice seemed to come from a long distance away.

"But what if it doesn't?" asked Kirby. Her own voice was a whisper and her eyes were closed before she could hear her mother's answer.

She asked the question again in the morning when Dr. Collins, the orthopedic surgeon who had set her leg, came in on his rounds.

"What if my leg doesn't mend?" she said.

"What a silly question," the doctor said lightly. "This is a simple break. I set fifty like it a year. Youngsters your age mend easily. You should be hopping around as good as new in a few months." He leaned over the bed to examine Kirby's foot, which was sticking out of the open end of the cast. "Wiggle your toes, please."

"But will I be able to dance?" Kirby persisted.

"I can't imagine why you wouldn't." The doctor leaned closer. "Now, stop asking questions a minute. I want you to wiggle your toes."

"I am," Kirby said.

"Listen to me, Kirby." The doctor was beginning to get impatient. "I want to see your toes moving."

"Then look at them!" Kirby was impatient also. She fought against the pain and tightened the muscles of her foot. "There, see? I am — I am wiggling them." She paused, disconcerted by the look on the doctor's face. "I am — aren't I?"

"Press your toes down," Dr. Collins told her. "I know it's painful, but you really must show me that you can do it."

"I am pressing them," Kirby said. "You mean, they're not moving?" A cold shaft of fear shot through her. "Something's wrong, isn't it? Other people with broken legs can move their toes."

"Well, yes. Most of them can." The doctor's round face was creased with a frown. "This is a bit unusual, but it may mean nothing. The nerves in your leg may just be numbed by the shock of the break." He patted her good leg reassuringly. "Let's not start worrying. Your toes will probably be wriggling all over the place by the time you're ready to leave us."

But they were not.

Kirby remained in the hospital four days. At the end of that time her toes were still completely motionless. They were beginning to look different too. They had drawn up slightly so that each one had a little curl to it.

The day she went home from the hospital was crisp and bright and sunny. Mr. Duncan came with Elizabeth to pick her up, as it was a two-man job getting her and the heavy cast in and out of the car. As they drove home along the beach road the salt wind blew across the sea grass so that it bent and swayed like a field of slender dancers.

"Won't it be good to be home again?" her mother asked her, and Kirby turned her head aside and did not answer.

Nancy and Brendon were waiting in the front yard. They rushed up to the car as though Kirby had been gone for years.

"Gee, what a cool cast!" Brendon exclaimed enthusiastically. "Can I be the first one to write my name on it?"

"You may not," said Kirby. She braced herself against the pain as Mr. Duncan lifted her gently out of the car.

Nancy said, "Oh, Kirby, I didn't mean for this to happen!" Her eyes were red as though she had been crying, and her face was very strange and pinched-looking.

"Nobody said you did," Kirby told her crisply. She did not want her sister weeping over her, or her mother's forced cheerfulness or any kind of emotion from anybody. She held tightly to Mr. Duncan's shoulder and was grateful that he did not talk to her as he carried her up the steps and into the house.

It was three weeks before they could go back to the doctor to have the cast opened. They were the longest, most miserable weeks that Kirby had spent in her life. With Nancy in school all day and their mother working, there was no one to talk to, and even if there had been, there was absolutely nothing she wanted to say.

Madame Vilar called several times, and Kirby would not speak to her.

"Tell her I'm asleep or something, won't you,

Mother?" she said when Elizabeth came to tell her that Madame was on the phone.

"But she is so concerned about you, dear," Elizabeth said. "And you have been so devoted to her. Wouldn't it make you feel better just to talk to her a moment?"

"No," Kirby said, so her mother went back to the phone and said that Kirby was sleeping.

Then many of her classmates and almost all the students at the dance studio sent notes and get-well cards. That was in a way even worse than phone calls.

"Here's one from Arlene White," Nancy said, wrinkling her nose in disgust. "Horrid thing! She sent a card with a picture of a ballerina on it!"

"Chuck it," Kirby told her bitterly. "I don't even want to see it." For the first time since she had seen her dance the Sugarplum Fairy, she felt envy instead of pity for Arlene.

The day that Kirby was to return to the doctor, Elizabeth took the morning off from work to drive her. When Dr. Collins came into the examination room he had another man with him.

"This is Dr. Sadock," he said, "a neurologist. He is going to run some tests on that leg of yours."

Kirby, who was stretched out flat on the examination table, nodded without speaking. She lay quiet while the cast was cut open by what appeared to be a small electric saw. When her leg was exposed she raised herself on her elbows to look down at it, and sank back, wishing that she had not done so. The leg was thin and white and covered with a growth of coarse black hair.

"Don't worry about that," Dr. Collins told her, noting her expression. "Body hair always grows heavily inside a cast. It will fall out within a week or so when it's back in the open air again."

Dr. Sadock was busy attaching a leather strap to Kirby's ankle. A cord ran from that to a machine that looked rather like a television set. Across the center of the screen ran a line of light.

"Now," he said, "I am going to prick your leg in various places with an electric needle. It will be a prick, that's all. It won't be particularly painful."

Kirby nodded. Her eyes were glued to the screen. She gave a start when the needle touched her for the first time. The light on the screen jumped and crackled like a bolt of lightning.

"Good," Dr. Sadock said. "Fine. A good response. That's exactly what we were hoping for."

He moved the leather strap to a new position and touched the leg again.

Kirby watched the screen as the needle stabbed her leg in first one spot and then another. Suddenly there was a prick, and the light on the screen remained motionless.

"That's it," she said. "Isn't it? There's something wrong there!"

Neither doctor answered her. Dr. Sadock tightened the strap on her ankle and pricked her again with the needle.

Still the light on the screen did not move.

"Here's our trouble," Dr. Sadock said in a low voice. He turned to the nurse who had been hovering in the back of the room. "Will you close the cast, please, Miss Martin? Then, Kirby, you can come out and join us.

Dr. Collins and I will be talking with your mother in my office."

Kirby was hardly aware of the nurse closing the cast. Later she would not remember being helped down from the table and handed crutches. What would stay in her mind forever was the moment of entering the doctor's office and seeing her mother turn toward her with tears shining in her eyes.

"What is it?" She did not ask her mother, but Dr. Collins. She did not want to make her mother be the one to say the words.

"Well, there is evidently some nerve damage, Kirby," the doctor told her carefully. "It's hard to tell exactly how much at this time."

"But the light did jump some !" Kirby said. She turned to Dr. Sadock. "It jumped in the beginning! I know! I saw it!"

"There are many different nerves in your leg, Kirby," the neurologist told her. "From the tests we made, it appears that only one of them is damaged. It's the big nerve that runs down the back of the leg, the one that feeds the toes. We don't know exactly how badly damaged this nerve is. There is a possibility that it may rejuvenate — that is, restore itself. That does sometimes happen. It is also possible —" He hesitated.

"Yes?"

"Well," the doctor said matter-of-factly, "if the nerve is completely severed, then there is no hope for it. We will simply have to face the fact that it is gone."

"And if it is —" Kirby could hardly bring out the words. "Does that mean I'll always be on crutches?"

"Of course it doesn't," said Dr. Sadock. "It is only

your toes that are affected. A person doesn't walk on her toes."

"Will I be able to dance?"

"I don't see why not," the doctor told her. "You won't be able to wear heels, of course — that would put too much pressure on your toes — but a tall girl like you is better off in flats anyway. You'll be dancing at your Christmas prom. You can promise your boyfriend that."

"That's not the kind of dancing I'm talking about," Kirby cried in desperation. "I mean real dancing! Ballet!"

"Darling," her mother broke in, "we'll just think positively. The nerve may grow back. The doctors say it may. We'll come back in about six weeks for more tests to see if things are improving. Meanwhile we'll just keep hoping. It's all we can do."

Kirby leaned upon her crutches and looked down. Her dress hung loose about her. Her arms stuck out, long and skinny, from the sleeves, and the good leg, lined up beside the cast, looked like a pipestem.

"For the first time," Kirby said softly, "I look like a dancer. And now it doesn't make any difference."

14

Nancy turned off her mind. Never again, she swore to herself, would she use it for anything but thinking.

I did this, she thought. I did this thing to Kirby.

The knowledge lay heavy within her like a kind of sickness. At night in bed she would play the scene over like the rerun of a movie — herself backed against the locker, looking upward — Kirby appearing on the landing, swaying, falling. Over and over she would see her sister lying in a crumpled heap at the foot of the stairs with her leg bent under her; she would hear her voice saying, "The Cecchetti exams — Ballet South — the scholarship —"

I'm evil, Nancy thought miserably. I am evil and dreadful and vicious. I'm like a witch with a terrible power! I put on curses!

In her nightmares she would hear her mind shrieking

the words that had caused the thing to happen: "Kirby can't go away — she just can't go — I won't let her!"

Well, Kirby was home now, all right. She would not be going to Atlanta or anywhere. And the Kirby who now lived with them was like no one they had ever known before.

"What you did to Miss Green was stinking," she snapped when Nancy tried to tell her the tale of the "dropsy" day. "I would think you could find something better to do with a gift like that than to frighten an old lady."

She was rude to her mother.

"I will *not* talk to people on the telephone or answer notes or anything," she told her flatly. "I just wish you'd stop hounding and nagging."

She was horridest of all to Brendon.

"You're a cheat," she said. "Here's Mother paying out her good money to give you music lessons, and you simply refuse to learn a thing. You never practice. You don't know the names of any of the notes. You're not learning anything at all."

"I know," Brendon said airily. One of the pleasant — and irritating — things about Brendon was that he never got angry. "I don't want to read music. It's a waste of time."

"You should be ashamed of yourself," Kirby told him. "To have a gift and not to develop it when you have a chance to — why, it's just plain criminal! If I were in your place I'd be studying every minute before school and after school. I'd be practicing scales and memorizing notes and . . . and . . ." She let the sentence fade off because she was not really certain what people did when they wanted to become musicians.

"Well, you're not in my place," Brendon said, "so what's it to you?" He stuck out his tongue at her and loped off, and a moment later they saw him through the window swinging down the driveway on his bicycle.

That evening after dinner he sat down at the piano and played all the pieces in Nancy's sheet music. After he was finished he got up and bowed, and let them see that the music was upside down. Kirby, who would once have thought that funny, was so furious that she left the room. They could all hear her climbing the stairs — thud, thump — thud, thump — hanging onto the railing with one hand and shoving herself up with the crutch on the other side.

In the suddenly silent living room the three other Garretts looked at each other helplessly.

It was Elizabeth who broke the quiet.

"I'm worried," she said. "I'm really worried. She's so — so — different. She won't see anyone, even Madame Vilar. She won't talk to any of her classmates on the phone. That nice boy, Paul something-or-other — he says he's the brother of one of your girl friends, Nancy — came by the other day with her school assignments, and she wouldn't see him. She hasn't opened a book either; at least, I don't think she has. What does she do with herself all day while I'm at work?"

"She mopes," Brendon said. "She feels sorry for herself." He did not say it in a mean way.

"I used to wish that Kirby couldn't dance." Nancy made the confession in a small shaky voice. "I thought then she would be with us more. I didn't realize how much of Kirby the dancing was. I feel so guilty now. It's as though with the dancing gone there isn't any Kirby left."

"Why should you feel guilty, dear?" Her mother was surprised. "You certainly had nothing to do with her taking that awful fall. And I don't agree. The dancing was just *part* of Kirby. The rest of Kirby, the daughter and sister part, was what was important to us. That's the part I'm afraid of losing." She paused.

"I think," she said slowly, "I am going to send her back to school."

"To school!" Nancy gasped, and even Brendon looked surprised.

"She won't go," he said. "If she won't talk to anybody now, you know she won't go to class. How could she drag around with that cast on? She couldn't even sit at a desk."

"If she can get herself up and down the stairs here at home," Elizabeth said, "she can manage to get around the school building. She can take a little footstool to prop her leg on, and Nancy can walk her to classes and carry it for her. I know it won't be easy, but I think it's necessary. She simply mustn't sit around here any longer getting more and more depressed."

Kirby objected violently when she heard her mother's decision.

"I won't," she said. "I just won't. I can't think about school now, not after what's happened to me! How could I possibly put my mind on studying when all my plans for my whole life have just been ruined!"

"I'm afraid you'll have to, dear," Elizabeth said with

unaccustomed firmness. "You have a whole life ahead of you, whether you can dance or not. The law says you have to go to school if you are physically able to, and Dr. Collins says you are. To stay home is truancy, and as your mother and legal guardian, I could be arrested for permitting it."

It was a statement that could not be argued with. The next day Kirby went to school. It was just as difficult as they had anticipated, and in some ways even more so.

Getting on and off the school bus proved to be so awkward that Elizabeth drove the girls to school every morning. She would stop in front of the side entrance, and then she and Nancy would get Kirby and the heavy cast out of the car. Then with Kirby on her crutches and Nancy carrying all the school books and a little folding stool, they would make their way slowly and painfully into the building and down the hall to Kirby's first class.

One thing Kirby flatly refused to do was to try the stairs.

"Once was enough," she said. "All I need now is to crack up the other leg."

So she only attended classes on the first floor, and during the periods in which she had second-floor classes she went instead to the study hall, where she sat, her eyes unfocused, seldom bothering to turn a page of whatever book happened to be lying open in front of her.

At first her teachers were sympathetic. They permitted her to come in late to classes and to be excused before the bell rang in order to have the hall clear for her trip through on her crutches.

As weeks went by, however, and Kirby seemed to be

making not the slightest effort to be part of the class, never volunteered to answer a question, left her test pages blank, did not take her books home or do the simplest homework assignments, their sympathy began to lessen.

Eventually it was replaced by irritation.

"We've had other students attend this school with broken limbs," Miss Line remarked in English class. "During football season especially there are always a couple of casualties. After a week or so they are swinging up and down the halls on their crutches, maneuvering stairs and doing beautifully. A broken leg certainly should not keep you from reading your assignments."

Miss Green was as nasty as always.

"You don't read with your leg, do you?" she asked in her most sarcastic voice.

"No, ma'am, you don't," Kirby said. She did not add any explanation. She simply looked at the teacher with flat, expressionless eyes as though she were seeing right through her.

"There's something terribly wrong with those Garrett children," Miss Green muttered later in the teachers' lounge to anyone who would listen. "They're not normal, either one of them. I've had difficult children in my classes over the years, but never any like these two. I'm just glad that I will be retiring before the third one gets to junior high age. From what I hear he's a perfect monster."

That day, when school let out, Elizabeth's car was not waiting for them in the faculty parking lot. Instead, Tom Duncan was there.

"Your mother phoned me," he said. "She has a flat tire and has had to call a garage to change it for her. She suggested that you call a taxi. I told her I'd bring you home myself."

"That's nice of you," Kirby said. She let herself be helped into the front seat of the car. Her face was pale and weary as it always was after a day of hauling herself around on crutches.

"You'll be getting a walking cast soon now, won't you?" Mr. Duncan commented. "That should be lighter and easier to handle."

Kirby nodded listlessly. Her face had its usual don't-care look.

Nancy handed her sister her books and said, "I don't need a ride, thank you. I'd rather walk."

"Get in, Nancy," Mr. Duncan told her. "You're going to have a ride whether you want one or not. I want to talk with both of you."

His tone was so firm that Nancy was startled. She glanced at Kirby and saw that she was equally surprised. In all the months they had known Tom Duncan he had never spoken to them any way except gently and politely.

"Get in," he said again, and to her own astonishment, Nancy found herself climbing into the back seat and pulling the door closed behind her.

For a moment they sat there in silence.

Then Mr. Duncan said, "A number of reports have come to my office, Kirby, about your attitude in your classes. I suppose you know that if you don't pull your marks up tremendously by the end of the next grading

period you stand a good chance of being forced to repeat your present grade."

"I suppose so," Kirby said. "It doesn't matter." She leaned back against the seat as though she were too tired to hold her head up.

"It may not matter to you," Mr. Duncan said, "but it does to your mother. She has had enough unhappiness lately without your adding to it. If you fail a grade she will feel that she's failed also."

"I don't see where our mother is any of your business," Nancy said. "Whatever problems she and Kirby have are between them."

"Your mother is my business," Mr. Duncan said quietly. "She always will be. I love her dearly, and it's very important to me to see her happy."

"I don't believe it," Nancy said, but she did. Suddenly all the things that she had been trying so hard not to admit to herself came snapping into place. "You can't love her," she said. "And anyway, she doesn't love you."

"She might have learned to," Tom Duncan said, "if you had let her. It would have been a good thing for your mother. It wouldn't have been too difficult for her either. She did love me once, you know."

"She did?" Kirby's eyes widened in astonishment. For the first time in weeks she actually looked interested. "You mean, way back when you were teen-agers?"

"And before that." Mr. Duncan spoke softly and his eyes held the look of remembering. "Your mother and I grew up together. We were playmates in grade school. We dated each other in high school. We had the same friends, the same interests, the same ideas of what would make a solid, happy life. I always planned to marry Elizabeth, and I don't think it ever occurred to her that she wouldn't marry me. Then, the year that she was a senior in high school, I went off to college."

"Yes?" Kirby was regarding him with fascination.

"That was the year," Tom Duncan said, "that a handsome young journalist came here to do a picture story. He hired some of the prettiest girls in town to work as models. Your mother was one of them." He paused. "When Richard Garrett went on to his next assignment, your mother went with him as his bride."

"How romantic!" Nancy said softly. Despite herself, she was enchanted by the story. "I guess there's nobody in the world who could compare to Dad!"

"He was handsome and dashing and adventurous," Mr. Duncan admitted. "He was all the things I wasn't, and Elizabeth fell in love with him. She wouldn't listen to anybody. Not to me — not to your grandmother —"

"You mean our grandmother didn't like Dad?" Kirby asked in astonishment. "I never knew anybody ever who didn't like him!"

"Oh, she liked him," Mr. Duncan said. "As you say, nobody could help it. But she knew that he wasn't right for your mother. Richard Garrett was made to be an adventurer, not a settled-down husband. And Elizabeth was made to be a mother and housewife. She tried — they both tried, I guess — but the strain, the constant uprooting were just too much for her. So the marriage ended, just as your grandmother predicted."

"What do you mean, she predicted it?" Nancy asked sharply. "You mean, to *you*?"

Mr. Duncan nodded. "When I came back from college I went to see her. I was heartbroken about losing Elizabeth. Your grandmother — she was a very special person — looked at me and said, 'Tommy, it isn't going to last. It can't last, and I know it. But when it ends and Elizabeth comes home again, I won't be here. It will have to be you who picks up the pieces.'"

"Well, you can't," Nancy told him determinedly. "Nobody can take Dad's place — not with Mother and not with us. They are going to get back together again. They simply *have* to."

"I doubt it," Tom Duncan said shortly. "But it doesn't matter. Your mother made a promise to you, Nancy, and she plans to keep it. And I — well, I'm not going to fight you. She's the one who would be hurt in the process, and we can't have that."

"You —" Nancy stopped, her mouth half open for more words of protest. "You're — giving up, then?"

"I said I was, didn't I?" His voice was quiet.

Kirby stared at him, her blue eyes incredulous.

"But I thought you said you loved her," she exclaimed in bewilderment. "How can you give up like that — without any reason? How can you give up the thing you want most in the world?"

"Because wanting doesn't make things so," Tom Duncan said gently. "We all can't have things exactly the way we would like them. There comes a time when we have to accept this fact and build our lives in new directions. Your mother has. And I can. And you —?"

He was not looking at Nancy, only at Kirby. Behind the pain in his eyes was something else — an odd look — a look you might expect to see in the eyes of a father.

"And you —?" he asked.

"Leave her alone!" Nancy cried. "You don't have any right to talk to her that way! Leave her alone; leave all of us alone!"

But Kirby was nodding.

"Yes," she said in a low voice, "I can too." And though her eyes were filled and shining, she did not cry.

15

Launching the boat was a good deal more difficult than building it. The worst of their problems was how to get it down to the water. Greg's workshop was a quarter mile inland, and the boat, by the time they had it completed, was eight feet long and at least a yard wide, and extremely heavy.

"We'll never be able to carry it," Brendon said. "We can just barely lift it. We should never have put all those orange crates on the back."

"We had to have those to hold the treasure," Greg reminded him. "We can't have it sliding off the deck and sinking! It's the seats that are heavy. We sure didn't have to have those."

"We have to sit on something, don't we?" The seats had been Brendon's idea. They were made from two chairs which they had found at the dump and had built to stand high like lookout towers. In his heart Brendon did have to admit that they were not necessities, but the thought of riding along high above the water was so enchanting that he knew even now that he could not possibly do without them.

"We've got to find something to wheel it on," he said. "Like a boat trailer."

"My dad's got a golf cart!" Greg's freckled face brightened. "That would do for one end. And I've got a pair of roller skates."

"That ought to do it," said Brendon. He eyed the boat appraisingly. "We can put the paddles and shovels on top of it and one of us guide and the other push from behind."

There was no question about where they were going to hold the launching. They had decided that weeks before. A hundred yards down the beach from Brendon's house there was a curve of rock which enclosed a little inlet piled with seaweed. People seldom swam there, even in the warm months, because of the fishy smell and the sharp shells. A boat that was launched there would not be seen from either direction until it was out past the rocks and well started on its journey toward the sand bar. Even then there would be little likelihood of detection, since people seldom strolled the beach on winter afternoons.

They attached the roller skates with a leather belt that Greg took from his father's closet.

"It's alligator," he said. "That should be plenty strong enough to hold them."

The back of the boat they propped on the golf cart.

Their most nerve-racking moments were spent in wheeling the boat out of the workshop and down the Russo driveway to the street. Dr. Russo was at his office and Mrs. Russo at bridge club, but there was always the chance of neighbors stopping them to ask what they were doing and where they were going. Once they reached the beach road, they relaxed a little. Several cars did pass them, and heads hung out windows with interested backward glances, but none of the cars contained people they knew.

"I sure hope your mom doesn't drive by right now," Greg said. "Isn't this about the time she gets off from work?"

"Not today," Brendon told him. "She took off early to drive Kirby to the doctor. She gets her cast off today and they're going to make some more tests on her leg."

"That should be good for at least an hour or so," Greg said knowledgeably. "How's old Kirby doing? She still compensating by turning her aggressions on you?"

"Nope," Brendon said. "She's done a real swing-around. She says nice things all the time and she smiles a big fake smile and she's even got a boyfriend. He comes over after dinner and they do their homework in front of the television."

"Kirby with a boyfriend!" Greg said. "Cripes! I'm sure glad I don't have sisters!" He generally preferred Kirby to Nancy, but choosing one girl over another was picking between evils. It was better to be without either of them.

They made good time on the beach road, but things became difficult when they had to leave it to start across the dunes. The sand was soft, and the wheels of the golf cart sank down into it. Once the skates came off and disappeared in the sand, and they had to dig them out again. At last they were forced to look for planks which they laid out to make runners like railroad rails. They would push the boat to the end of them and pull the planks out and lay them in front for the next stint.

It was tiring work, and it was with relief that they finally reached the damp sand near the water's edge.

"It took longer than we planned," Brendon said, looking at his watch. He raised his eyes and squinted out at the water, shining silver in the slanted rays of the afternoon sun.

"Do you think we should wait till tomorrow?" Greg asked.

"Tomorrow's Saturday," Brendon said. "You know — dumb piano lesson."

"And your mom home," Greg said. "And my mom home. And Nancy bugging us. And people on the beach. You know they do come and walk on the beach on Saturdays even when it's too cold to swim."

"Yeah," Brendon said. His eyes were still on the water. The white streak of sand which was the bar rose temptingly against the horizon, and there was still plenty of sunlight and the tide hadn't begun to turn yet.

"Come on," he said. "We'd better get started."

They had to lift the boat and carry it to get it into the water. The rudder scraped on the shells, and for a moment they thought they might have disconnected it. Brendon, who was supporting the bow, staggered backward beneath the weight of the pilot's seat. He felt the cold water lap through his tennis shoes and saw Greg's face grow red with exertion as he carried the stern.

"We're not going to make it," Greg gasped, and then suddenly, miraculously — they *had* made it! The boat was in the water!

Releasing his hold, Brendon straightened and let the waves take over.

"She floats!"

"Boy, does she! She's great!" cried Greg.

"She's better than great!" shouted Brendon. "She's beautiful!"

Working quickly, they loaded the shovels and paddles into the orange crates.

"All aboard!" Greg cried and swung himself onto the deck.

Brendon gave the boat a hard shove and threw himself onto the stern. Icy water splashed his legs, and a wave washed over the deck, soaking his shirt. Shivering with chill and excitement, Brendon grabbed one of the paddles and pushed it against the sandy bottom. The boat swung sideways, and Greg caught the second paddle and pushed on the other side.

The boys poled until the water grew too deep and then began to paddle. The boat moved further and further out until it had passed beyond the jut of rock. Now when they turned to look over their shoulders they could see the entire beach stretched long and empty behind them.

"Hey, this is the life!" Greg's red hair was standing up straight in the salt breeze.

"Let's never come back!" shouted Brendon. "Let's go on forever!"

Excitement surged within him, high and bright and feverish. He grinned into the sun and felt the wind cold against his teeth. For a moment he wished that Greg was not here with him. If he were alone he would head for Mexico or even farther. He would keep on going until he reached the end of the world!

But that would be another time, another day. Now he grasped his paddle tightly and brought it hard through the water in fast, strong strokes. The sand bar grew larger, rushing toward them like a thin white ship.

"Hang on!" yelled Brendon. "We're coming in for a landing!"

The moment the bow touched sand he was over the side.

"Help me," he cried to Greg who was trying to collect the shovels. "The current's real strong here!"

Hurriedly Greg slid off the side of the deck to join him. Gasping and shivering, they hauled the boat up onto the sand spit.

The shore looked surprisingly far away when they gazed back at it. They could see Mr. Duncan's cottage with its dock out in front. The roof of the Garrett house rose over the top of a dune, looking as though it were perched upon it. Past the beach the sea grasses moved like a rippling forest.

The light lay low across the water between.

"We won't have much time," Brendon said. "We'd better start digging."

Greg glanced down at the sand at their feet. "Where

shall we do it? Did your mom say what part the stuff was buried on?"

"For rats' sake," said Brendon. "If folks knew that they'd have dug it up years ago. Let's start in the middle and work out on both directions."

"That could take a year," Greg said, but he got the shovels. They started their hole in the center of the bar as Brendon had suggested.

"What kind of treasure do you think it will be?" Greg asked after they had been working a few moments. "Pieces of eight and stuff? Jewelry, maybe?"

"Gold and silver," Brendon said. "They stole it off ships, you know. And I bet there's a lot or they wouldn't have bothered to bury it."

"What are you going to do with your share?" Greg asked him. "That is, if we find it?"

"Oh, we'll find it," said Brendon. "It just may take a while." Until Greg's question, he had not thought past the thrill of the actual digging. Spending the treasure was something he had not really considered.

"I'll give it to my mom, I guess," he said finally. "She can buy herself clothes and stuff, and maybe some books for Nancy."

"I'm going to get myself a car," Greg said. "And an airplane. And flying lessons."

"Hey, cool!" Brendon was disgusted with himself for not having considered further. "I'll do that too with part of it. Mom doesn't need all that many new dresses. She's got some pretty nice ones already."

They stopped talking then to save their breath for digging. The task was proving more difficult than either boy had anticipated. The sand was wet and heavy, and the water level was so near the surface that the holes began to fill up almost immediately. Then the sand from the edges would slide down into the water.

"What we need to do," Brendon said finally, "is brace the sides like they do in mine shafts. We should have brought some pieces of wood along for braces."

"We can use the orange crates," Greg suggested. Straightening, he leaned on his shovel and turned to look at the boat. "Say, the tide's coming in darned fast. The stern's afloat."

Brendon sent his shovel down once more into the hole he was digging.

"Greg!" he said. "Greg, I hit something!"

"You did!" Greg yanked his gaze back from the boat. "What sort of something?"

"It's metal, I think!" Brendon was down on his knees, dipping into the hole with his hand. His heart was pounding with excitement. "Oh, rats, the sides are caving in again! Hurry, Greg, get the orange crates! We can knock them apart with the shovels!"

Dropping his spade, Greg dashed over to the boat where it sat bobbing, half in, half out of the water. As he clambered on board, Brendon cried, "It *is* metal! I can just touch it with my fingers!"

"Darned crates! We nailed them on too tight!" Greg began wrestling with the slat wood boxes. Suddenly he gave a sharp cry. "Hey, Bren, I'm drifting!"

"You're what?" Brendon raised his head. To his horror he saw the boat with his friend aboard it a good three yards out past the end of the sand bar.

"Pole it back!" Brendon yelled. "Where's the paddle?"

"Over here!" Greg scrambled to the other side of the boat. He caught up the paddle and thrust it into the water. "I can't touch bottom! It's too deep!"

"Then paddle!" Brendon was standing now, the hole in the sand forgotten.

Desperately Greg began to use the oar on his one side. The boat swung around in an arc.

The distance between the boys was growing every second.

"The current's too strong!" Greg shouted. "I can't handle the boat myself! It's too heavy for one person."

"Oh, great!" Brendon contemplated plunging into the water and trying to swim. Even as he considered it he knew he could never reach the boat. The current was pulling it toward the open sea.

"Paddle on the far side!" Brendon called. "Switch back and forth! Try to keep it moving in a straight line!"

"I can't!" Greg cried. His face was contorted with strain.

It was too late now to even attempt to swim.

Brendon stood quiet, feeling the last faint warmth of the afternoon sun upon his shoulders, watching the boat draw further and further away.

Then suddenly he grew aware of the lap of water against his feet. The tide was coming in.

16

Nancy was home alone when the letter arrived.

She had almost gone with her mother and Kirby.

"Come with us, dear," Elizabeth had suggested. "We can stop somewhere afterward and celebrate. We can get ice cream sodas or something. My goodness, your sister doesn't get a cast off every day!"

"Do come, Nance," Kirby had echoed. "We can call this my coming-out party!"

She might really have gone if Kirby had not come forth with that. There was something about Kirby being cheerful which was even worse than Kirby being sorry for herself.

The change in Kirby had taken place in Mr. Duncan's car. From that moment on she seemed to have become a different person.

The first thing she had done when she reached home that day was to phone Madame Vilar.

"I'm sorry for not calling you back before," she said. "Please thank all the kids for the lovely cards and things." Then she had sat there holding the receiver, listening, for a long time.

"Thank you," she had said finally. "I might like that — sometime. Not right now, but sometime. I'll — I'll think about it."

"What did she say?" Nancy asked when her sister had hung up the phone.

"She offered me a job," Kirby said, "helping teach at the studio. Like Miss Nedra does, and Miss Julie. I wouldn't have to actually dance or anything. I could just teach and use a demonstrator to show the steps."

"Would you really like that?" Nancy asked her in surprise. It was very hard to imagine Kirby teaching.

"I suppose I might," Kirby said, "when I've had a chance to get used to the idea a little. After all, I'll have to do *something*, won't I?" She smiled a quick, bright smile and went out to help in the kitchen.

At school the change in Kirby was even more miraculous. For the first time she seemed to look around her and see the other students. Instead of dreaming through lunch hour, she deliberately seated herself at crowded tables. She joined in conversation and made little jokes and listened attentively to her classmates' gossip. Before long girls who had previously regarded her as "stuck-up" began to refer to her as "sweet" and "nice" and "funny." The magnetism which had always made her dancing so special was irresistible when she turned it on for her fellow students.

Her schoolwork improved as she began to do her assignments. She looked alert in class and kept her eyes on her teachers. She even allowed Barbara's brother, Paul, to carry her books and footstool through the halls for her and to come over in the evenings and help her study.

"It'll save your having to do it," she said to Nancy. "Besides, it's time I started to think about boys. The other girls do, and if I can't be a dancer, I guess I should plan to get married. That way I can have a daughter and *she* can be a ballerina."

To Elizabeth the change was a kind of miracle.

"I was right," she said, "to send her back to school." The lines of worry which had begun to show in her face since Kirby's accident smoothed away. "She must have just been going through an adjustment period. Thank goodness she's found herself now and begun to be happy."

Nancy snatched gratefully at her mother's words. Maybe, it's going to work out all right, she thought. The things she had always dreamed of for Kirby were now beginning to materialize. She was popular, she was sociable, she was paying attention to boys. She was talking about teaching and marriage, just like any other pretty teen-age girl.

Her life isn't ruined at all, Nancy kept telling herself. When she gets used to it she'll love being nice and normal. She'll be *glad* someday that she didn't waste her whole life flitting around the stage.

The thought was comforting, and if she repeated it to herself often enough it made her feeling of guilt more endurable.

She was careful when she was with her sister never to open her mind to Kirby's. The one time she had, a terrible feeling had poured in on her, a thick, gray fog of emotion so heavy and strange that Nancy had nearly strangled.

She can't really be feeling that, she had thought frantically. Not and act so gay all the time! It must just be left over somehow from the way she felt before.

From then on, though, Nancy had kept her mind tightly closed. She knew that she could not bear to face that grayness again.

It was because of this that she did not go with Kirby and her mother to the doctor and was at home alone, trying to read, when the special-delivery letter arrived. It was addressed to all of them. She stood holding it a moment, staring down at her father's bold, black handwriting, thinking, he's safe, he must be all right and safe to have written this. My feeling was wrong! He's all right and safe!

She thought, I should wait until the others get home so we can open it together.

Even as she thought it, her hands were tearing open the envelope. She drew the pages out and spread them flat and read the opening lines:

Dear kids —

This will come as a surprise to you, but I hope that after you get used to the idea you'll be pleased about it. Maggie Courtney and I were married last weekend.

Maggie Courtney and I were married last weekend!

Nancy reread the words with a feeling of bewilderment. It was a joke, of course. Her father, married! Impossible! He's being funny, she told herself. Further on he'll say he's joking.

But as her eyes flew down the page, and line followed line, there was no reference to a joke. Maggie, he said, was a fine woman, a topnotch correspondent, a great photographer. "Your mother has met her," he wrote, "and will tell you all about her." Maggie had never been married. She had always been afraid that to marry meant that she would have to give up her career and be tied down as a housewife. "I thought that I would never marry again," wrote Richard Garrett, "because my kind of life is not one to make a home-loving woman happy. But Maggie is not a home lover, and I am not a man who needs a housewife. In our own strange way, we fit each other perfectly. My hope is that your mother is as lucky as I am and soon finds the person who can give her the happiness she deserves."

He would be home in the summer as originally planned, he said, bringing Maggie with him. He knew that they would like her.

It was not a joke, then. It was true — it was horribly true! *Maggie Courtney and I were married last weekend!* Nancy turned back to those first incredible words and forced herself to read and reread them. Her father was married. There was no chance now that he would ever come back to her mother.

There was never any chance, she realized now. Never even in the beginning. She had been fooling herself into believing something that could not possibly be.

Oh, Dad, she cried silently, how could you do this! How could you do it!

With all of her mind she reached out to her father. For the first time since Kirby's accident, she let herself open completely. Dad! she cried. Dad! — and her mind was stretched wide in all directions, a great, groping emptiness, aching with the shock of loss, screaming, Dad, Dad, come back to us, tell us it isn't true!

And into this openness came a voice calling, "Nancy!"

For a moment Nancy was too startled to comprehend. It's Dad, she thought, but it was not her father's voice. Kirby? Was it Kirby? She found Kirby in an instant. She was sitting in the doctor's waiting room, leafing through a magazine, trying to pretend that she was reading. Elizabeth was seated across from her. Neither of them was thinking about Nancy.

But if not her father or her mother or her sister, that left only Brendon. Surely it wouldn't be *Brendon* — and at the thought of her brother a feeling of cold shot through her, so sudden and violent that it left her ill and shivering. It *was* Brendon! Something was wrong with him! Terribly wrong!

But how could there be? Wasn't he over at Greg's house? He was always at Greg's house.

Dropping her father's letter onto the coffee table, Nancy hurried over to the telephone. The Russo number was scrawled on the front of the directory in Brendon's own sloppy handwriting.

Nancy dialed it, and after a moment the maid's voice answered, "Russo residence."

"Hello," Nancy said. "This is Nancy Garrett. Could I speak to my brother?"

"Mr. Brendon's not here," the maid said. "Leastways, I don't think so. He and Mr. Greg came through here earlier and ate up half the cake I made for dinner. Then they run off somewhere. They ought to be back soon, though. Mrs. Russo likes Greg home before it gets dark."

"Do you think they told Greg's mother where they were going?" asked Nancy.

"No, Miss," the maid said. "I'm sure not. Mrs. Russo was out at her bridge club till just a few minutes ago. Would you like to speak to her?"

"No, I guess not, thanks," said Nancy. Slowly she lowered the receiver and replaced it on the hook.

Now she was really beginning to be worried. She thought, *Brendon!* She tried to find him with her mind, but he slid past her, as he had a way of doing lately, flickering like light and shadow, a will-o'-the-wisp. Like his father, he could not be grasped and held.

I'm being silly, she told herself. Nothing is ever wrong with Brendon.

She went back to the coffee table and picked up their father's letter, but strangely now she could not focus her mind upon it. What a moment ago had seemed so important was only words on a sheet of paper. After a moment, she laid it down again and left it there and went out onto the porch.

Standing looking out toward the sea, she shivered a little in the cool salt breeze. The sun was low in the sky, resting on the top of a dune, screened by the sea grass so that the golden afternoon light was diffused and soft.

Nancy shivered again, and this time it was not because of the wind. Something is wrong, she thought. Something is very, very wrong —

And then it hit her. It came like a bolt, a shock, a stab of ice, a churning, sickening terror, a voice screaming through her, so piercing that there was no other sound, no other reality in the world. *"Nancy! Nancy!"*

"Bren!" She cried his name. She could see him now, clear and sharp before her eyes, as real to her mind as her mother and Kirby had ever been. He was silhouetted against the sun so that she could not see his face. His light hair was plastered against his head, and there was water — water — all around him.

Brendon, she thought, he's going to drown! Brendon is drowning!

She moved so quickly then that later, thinking back on it, she was not to remember having moved at all. In an instant she was in the house with the telephone in her hand dialing a second number.

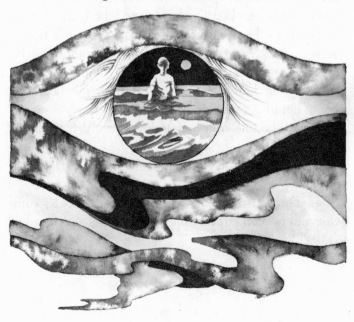

The voice answered immediately, as though it had been waiting for her.

"Mr. Duncan," she gasped, "this is Nancy. You've got to come fast! Brendon's drowning!"

"He's what?" There was a startled sound from the man at the other end of the line. "Where is he? Where are you? What's happened?"

"I'm at home. Mother and Kirby are out. Bren's out in the water. I don't know where — I think, in a boat —"

"You get out of that house and start running," Mr. Duncan said. "It'll be faster than my coming to get you. I'll meet you at the dock in front of my place."

"All right," Nancy said, and was running even before she reached the porch.

She flew down the steps and across the dunes with the soft sand squeaking beneath her feet and the sun orange in her eyes and that voice screaming in her brain, over and over again. *"Nancy! Nancy!"*

When she reached the hard sand, she could see up the beach to the dock in front of Mr. Duncan's house. He was already out there, untying the motor boat. By the time she was on the dock itself, the motor was started. Tom Duncan reached up from the boat and caught her under the arms and lifted her in.

"Okay," he said in a low, tight voice. "Where do we go?"

"Out there," Nancy said, and she pointed straight to sea.

Mr. Duncan turned the rudder and the boat swung wide and headed out into open water. The sky ahead of them had burst into sunset. Orange flames sprang from the water to echo in the clouds.

"Where?" Mr. Duncan asked again, and Nancy said, "To the bar."

"There isn't any bar," Mr. Duncan said quietly, "when the tide's in."

"It can't be," Nancy said — and as she said it, she could see that he was right. The sun's last rays reflected in the water, unbroken streaks of gold and flame. There was no rim of white sand rising above them.

"But it can't be," Nancy whispered. "It just can't!"

"You'd know," Tom Duncan said. "If it were too late, you'd know it. You knew he was out here. You'd know if he suddenly — wasn't."

"I don't know what I do know," Nancy sobbed.

Clutching the side of the boat with both hands, she tried to see through the glare of light on water, of sea and sky. In her head the voice was screaming, screaming — and then — it was not in her head, it was in her ears.

Weak in her ears — "Nancy!"

"There he is," Tom said. "There!"

A tiny black spot. A bit of driftwood. A fish. They drew closer, and an arm rose, waving to them. They were closer, closer — Nancy could see the shape of his head.

"Brendon!" she cried, and then they were beside him.

Nancy gazed down over the side of the boat into the tilted green eyes of her brother. They were red now with salt, and the soft hair was plastered darkly to his head, and the face was white beneath its tan, and the dimple — unbelievable as it was, the dimple was flashing in the smooth, wet cheek, and Brendon's voice, weary, gasping, half strangled, was trying to make words.

Tom bent over and caught him by the shoulders and dragged him up and into the boat like a grounded fish.

"It sure took you one heck of a long time to get here," said Brendon.

17

"How the devil did you get out here?"

Tom Duncan's voice grated with a mixture of anger and relief.

To Nancy it was an echo of her own feelings exactly. Looking at Brendon, small and sopping, sprawled out upon the floor of the boat, she could hardly keep from throwing her arms around him. At the same time she had an almost irresistible desire to hit him. Never had she loved him more or been more furious at him.

"Don't tell us you swam," she said. "You couldn't have. Besides, you've got all your clothes on. You'd never have gone swimming that way."

"I'm not wearing my shoes," Brendon said self-righteously. He coughed and shook his head sideways to get the salt water out of his ears. "We came out in a boat, Greg and me, but the boat took off on us. It got caught in the current and Greg wasn't fast enough to pole it back."

"Greg?" Tom Duncan asked. "You mean Greg Russo was with you? Then where is he?"

"Out there someplace." Brendon motioned toward the passage to the open sea. He pulled himself to a sitting position and turned his gaze out across the crimson water. "We'd better get out there. I bet he's scared."

"Not in this boat, we can't," Tom said. "It's almost dark." He too was staring toward the passage and his face was set and worried. "That's open sea out there. This boat is too small to handle it. What sort of boat does Greg have?"

"A good one," Brendon told him. "It's made for weather. It floats like anything, and we've got it caulked up good with chewing gum and a layer of glue on top of that."

"You've got it caulked —" Tom began to repeat the sentence and broke off in the middle as the full meaning of the words swept over him. He swung around to face Brendon in horror. "You *built* the boat? Greg is out there in the Gulf — with night coming — *in a boat you built yourselves?*"

"It's a good boat," Brendon insisted. "The deck's real solid. We've got crates across the back of it so he won't wash off. If a big wave hits he can always stick his feet in the crates and —"

The roar of the motor cut off his words as Tom Duncan gave a frantic yank to the rope that brought the engine into life. Nancy, in the bow, clung tightly to her seat as the boat lurched into a sharp arc, almost throwing her over the side.

In the stern, Tom's face was a grim silhouette against the fading pink of the sky.

"You kids!" he growled. "You darned fool, crazy idiots! You need a keeper, every one of you! *Glue and chewing gum!*"

His voice came out in a hoarse kind of croak.

But Brendon is safe, Nancy told herself. This time at least. The boy out there is Greg, it isn't Brendon.

The selfishness of the thought horrified her, but she couldn't fight it. The memory of Brendon's voice screaming from the water still filled her heart with echoes. She did not want Greg to drown. She hoped and prayed that he could be rescued. But at least it wasn't Brendon — it wasn't Brendon.

This is how Mother felt, she realized suddenly, during all those years with Dad. This is what she meant when she talked about being a nesting pigeon married to an eagle. For the first time she found herself understanding something of what it might be to be the one who was left behind to love and worry.

It would take a strong person, she thought. A really strong person. I hope when Brendon grows up and marries it will be to somebody tough enough to take it.

The sun was down before they reached the dock. The sky had dulled to a faint rose and stars dotted it with tiny pinpricks of light. By the time that Nancy and Brendon had secured the boat and crossed the dunes to Tom's cottage, night had closed down, flat and dark. When they looked out toward the horizon there was no telling the water from the sky.

Tom leaped from the boat almost before the engine had stopped running. When they reached the living room he was already setting the telephone receiver back on the hook.

"Greg was lucky," he said quietly. "He got home safely. I'd say, Brendon, that between the two of you, you boys have had enough luck to last a lifetime."

"I told you the boat was a good one," Brendon said. There was a note of pride in his voice. "It could make it in the ocean."

"Thank God it wasn't put to that test," Tom Duncan told him. "It grounded at the point right at the edge of the passage. Greg hiked back to the highway and phoned his father. When I talked to the Coast Guard Station just now they were just getting ready to send a patrol boat out to search for you."

"For me!" Brendon exclaimed. "Gosh!" For an instant he seemed abashed. Then his face brightened. "Do you think it'll be in the papers?"

"I wouldn't be surprised," Tom Duncan said dryly. "Now get into the bathroom and get yourself dried off before you come down with pneumonia. There's a robe hanging on the back of the door; you can put that on. And stop being so cocky. You weren't brave, you were stupid. If your sister didn't have the gift she does, you would be food for fish by this time."

"I could have kept swimming," Brendon said peevishly, but he did as directed. Halfway across the room he paused and turned accusingly to Nancy. "I thought you weren't going to tell anybody about your ESP thing. You made Kirby and me promise to keep it a secret."

"I didn't have to tell Mr. Duncan," Nancy said. "He just knew. He's always known, even after I flunked the card test."

"That is actually the point at which I became certain." Tom shoved some fishing gear off the overstuffed chair by the window.

"Sit down," he said. "You look as though you need to. You've had quite a workout this evening. You must be exhausted."

"I — I guess — I am," Nancy said shakily, and suddenly was. Her legs seemed to fold beneath her as she sank gratefully into the chair and leaned back in it. She watched Mr. Duncan as he crossed to the sofa. This was the first time she had ever seen him in his own home and he seemed different here somehow, bigger, more in command of things.

Curiously she glanced about her at the cluttered front room of the cottage. It did not look like a place she would have expected a school counselor to live in. A pipe rack sat on the bookcase and on the table at the end of the sofa there was a pile of magazines on an assortment of subjects — politics, sports, photography, even engineering. A hunting rifle hung on the wall by the door and a stuffed tarpon resided over the mantel. A fishing pole leaned against a chair as though its owner had been called away in the process of repairing it.

"What do you mean," she asked, "that that was when you were certain? I guessed all the cards wrong. I called the red ones black and all the black ones red."

"That's just it," Tom said. "That was a dead giveaway. The odds against doing that are just as great as the odds against naming all the cards correctly. It was pretty good proof that you were clairvoyant and trying not to let anyone know about it."

"If you guessed that, then Dr. Russo must have too."

Nancy regarded him in growing bewilderment. "Why didn't one of you say something? When Mother told Dr. Russo I didn't want to take more tests he didn't keep on any further. He just let the whole thing go as if he didn't think it important."

"What else could he do?" Tom Duncan asked her. "This gift is your own. It's your property and nobody else's. There isn't anyone in the world who can force you to share it with science if you don't choose to."

"You mean all those people who took part in experiments did it because they wanted to?" Nancy was incredulous. "They thought it was fun, acting as guinea pigs?"

"Maybe some of them did," said Mr. Duncan. "They could have enjoyed feeling important. Many others liked the idea of contributing to the world's store of knowledge. Still others wanted a chance to develop their gift to the fullest potential. Through working with doctors in their studies they could compare their abilities with those of others."

"I'd like to know how other people use theirs," Nancy admitted despondently. "It seems like all I do is make a lot of unhappiness. Miss Green — well, I don't feel so bad about that one. She deserved to worry about having dropsy. But Kirby — I did a terrible thing to Kirby. And to you and Mother. You probably guessed that, didn't you? I've been pushing against the two of you every minute."

"Your problem," Tom Duncan said wryly, "is that you are a born manager of the people around you. If you didn't have ESP you'd still probably be one. You ought

178

to take a few lessons from your grandmother. She didn't try to arrange other people's lives for them."

"She didn't?" Nancy asked him. "Even if she loved them? Even if she knew, just *knew,* they were making awful mistakes?"

"She could have stopped your parents' marriage," Mr. Duncan reminded her quietly. "She knew, though, that your mother's life was her own possession. So she sat back and waited — and loved her — and understood her. If she hadn't, you and Kirby and Brendon wouldn't be here."

"I'm hungry. Do you have some food? Cookies or something?" Brendon appeared in the doorway wrapped in a terrycloth bathrobe. His cheeks were flushed and his eyes shone as green as emeralds. His hair had dried and fluffed up around his head like yellow feathers.

"I think I'd better get the two of you home," Tom Duncan told him. He started to say something more but his words were interrupted by the shrill blast of the telephone. The sound shot through the room like the scream of a terrified voice.

"That's Mother," Nancy said. "She's just got home with Kirby. They've come into the house, and nobody's there, and they're worried. She's calling *you* because — I don't know why exactly —"

"Don't you really?" Mr. Duncan gave her a long look. "I think you do know. I think, little manager, that you just don't want to accept it."

He picked up the receiver and his voice changed in that special way that it always did when he spoke to Elizabeth.

"Hello, dear," he said. "The kids are here with me. You don't have to worry." He paused while the voice on the other end of the line asked something.

"How did I know it was you?" He grinned and flashed a glance at Nancy. "Why, I guess it must have been ESP that told me."

"*My* ESP," Nancy said possessively, and Brendon stifled a giggle.

"Just a moment," Tom Duncan said into the phone. "She's right here. I'll get her." He held the receiver out to Nancy. "Your mother says Kirby wants to talk with you. She says it's important. It's something that she wants to tell you herself."

Nancy got up quickly and crossed the room to the telephone.

"Hi, Kirby," she said, and was allowed to get no further.

Her sister's voice came leaping over the wire in a rush of excitement.

"Nancy, guess what? Guess what happened! I got my cast off!"

"Well, sure," Nancy said in surprise. "That's what you went to the doctor for, wasn't it?" It seemed a million years ago that her mother and Kirby had left the house. So many things had happened in the meantime.

"I've got so much to tell you," Nancy said. "Brendon almost drowned, and we took Mr. Duncan's boat to get him, and there is a letter from Dad —"

"Nancy, listen to me!" Kirby interrupted. "Please, listen! This is important! They took more tests and, Nance, the light line wiggled! They stuck a needle in my foot and the light on the screen started jumping!

The nerve isn't dead at all! It's growing! Oh, *Nancy!*"

She was crying — Kirby, who never cried. Emotion came rushing through the wire, joy, wonder, relief, so strong and overpowering that it was all that Nancy could do to hang onto the receiver as the force of it struck her.

"Then you'll dance?" she asked.

"Dance? Of course, I'll dance! Well, first there'll be therapy. And catching up. And practice. It'll take months to get back the way I was again, maybe even years. By the time I get to Atlanta I may be the oldest ballerina in the troupe, but I'll make it, Nance! I'll get there!"

"All that work," Nancy said doubtfully. "Is it really worth it? I thought you were learning to like the idea of being — well — like other people. You've got so many friends now, and Paul —"

"Paul!" Kirby gave a disdainful snort. "Oh, really! Paul doesn't know royale ouverte from entrechat! I've got to call Madame Vilar now, Nance. I'll talk to you later."

Nancy hung up and turned to Tom Duncan.

"She'll have the life she wants," she said. "I didn't wreck it. But all the make-up work — it'll take her so long now — and I'm responsible —"

"You?" Tom said. "Why should you feel responsible?"

"Because I'm the one who made her fall." For the first time Nancy spoke the terrible words aloud. "I have this power — I can make things happen to people — like a witch —"

"Don't be ridiculous," Tom said. "No one is that

powerful. You're not a witch, Nancy, or God, or a magician. You're a twelve-year-old girl with a sensitivity that is tuned a little higher than that of other people. You didn't make Kirby fall any more than you started her nerve ends mending."

"Then why —" Nancy began in bewilderment.

"Your sister fainted. It would have been strange if she hadn't. Any growing girl who skips breakfast and lunch in order to lose weight —"

"Do you think that's what happened?" Nancy's voice was shaking.

For the first time since she had met him she looked at Thomas Duncan. Past the colorless hair, the glasses, the thin, unhandsome face, she looked into the man himself. He was not her father and never would be or could be, but still, oddly, now he was a part of her life — and Kirby's — and Brendon's. And, most of all, Elizabeth's.

Slowly, deliberately, inch by careful inch, she let the bars down and let the feel of the man come into her. The strength. The warmth. The kindness.

"Do you think that's really what happened?" she asked.

"I don't just think it, I *know*," Tom said. "Kirby told me herself on the way to the hospital."

Epilogue

. . . and so they lived happily ever after, or at least, for good long lifetimes.

Kirby became a famous dancer and went to live in London.

Nancy married quite young and had five children. She always knew where they all were and exactly what they were doing.

Brendon tried his hand at a number of things and finally became a helicopter pilot. He never did anything with his music except occasionally to fill in playing piano in nightclubs.

After Thomas Duncan and Elizabeth Garrett were married, they had one more child, a daughter. Her name was Lois, and she was born with the gift of story-telling.